MORE BOOKS BY
DAISY PRESCOTT

Love with Altitude:
Next to You
Crazy Over You
Wild for You
Up to You (2018)

Modern Love Stories:
We Were Here (prequel to Geoducks)
Geoducks Are for Lovers
Wanderlust
Happily Ever Now (2018)

Wingmen:
Ready to Fall
Confessions of a Reformed Tom Cat
Wingmen
(a boxed set of *Ready to Fall &*
Confessions of a Reformed Tom Cat)
Anything but Love
Better Love
Small Town Scandal

Bewitched:
Bewitched
A magical short set in Salem, Massachusetts
Spellbound
A magical sequel to Bewitched
Enchanted
A magical continuation (coming October 2017)

WILD FOR YOU

DAISY PRESCOTT

Cover Design by ©SM Lumetta

Cover photos: ©Studio Firma; ©Rawpixel

Editing: There for You Editing

Proofreading: Proofing Style

Interior Design & Formatting: Type A Formatting

For the wild ones

I'm sick of their city games
I crave a real wild man.
Lady Gaga

ONE

ZOE

"THE BEST WAY to get over a man," Mara says, lifting her margarita, "is—"

Sage interrupts her. "To go to the rodeo and get your ho down with a cowboy."

My best friend proudly grins at her new solution for heartbreak. Breakup solidarity blue streaks the tips of her blond hair, a new color from her typical pink.

"That's not what I was going to say, but I like it if ho down means you'll ride a cowboy." Mara lifts her glass higher and her gold curls bounce with her enthusiasm. "To big belt buckles!"

"Aren't all cowboys bowlegged and reek of horses?" I wrinkle my nose. "Unwashed, missing teeth. Chewing tobacco. Sleeping outdoors on the ground. Eating cold canned beans. Out of the can. With a knife or a twig."

Three sets of eyes stare unblinking at me.

"What?" I pull on my braid. "I've seen a few Western movies."

Mae is the first to speak. "Zoe, you're kidding, right?"

"I'm from Chicago. We don't really do the whole Wild West, big belt buckle thing. Or cowboy boots. Or the hats."

Sage speaks and I'm hoping she's going to back me up. "We're not in Illinois anymore, best friend of mine. This is the American West."

"Exactly my point." I agree with her on the geography lesson.

"Cowboys are hot. How have you never been to the rodeo in Snowmass? What's wrong with us that this isn't our weekly thing? Pink Taco Tuesdays and Rodeo Wednesdays." Margarita sloshes over the edge of Mae's glass as she lifts it in a toast to our foursome. The four of us have become a tight squad over the past six months.

"Wild Women Wednesdays has a better ring to it." Mara sets down her drink with a loud clunk on the wood table. She only does this when she has something important to say or she has to go to the ladies' room. "I have a confession. I've never been to a rodeo either."

"You're from New England. You're forgiven," Mae says.

"Horses make me nervous." Mara stares at the table, twisting a blond curl nervously around her finger.

"We need to change this. As soon as possible." Mae's dark eyes blaze with mischief as she raises her glass again. "To getting back on the horse. And by horse, I mean man."

"Cheers," Mara says. "Let me tell you from experience . . . the man you think you should end up with isn't always the man you need. See, the problem is you're thinking with your brain. Checking off lists and putting things in boxes. Silly human. The heart, not the brain, is where love lives. Sure, we can convince ourselves we're in love. But not for long. My ex, Geoffrey, was smart, nice, kind, and great on paper. Zero zings. Jesse and I don't line up on paper, yet we work."

"Zings?" I ask.

"All of them." She stares into space with a soft, dreamy expression on her face. "And those laser noises. Pew pew pew.

In my pants."

"Thanks for sharing. If the burning laser sensation lasts for more than a few hours, you might need a special cream," Mae says, frowning while the rest of us laugh. She holds the scowl for about ten seconds before cracking up.

"Not sure I've had zings." I finish my drink and think about ordering another one. We're sitting on the deck of Agave, under the heat lamps. Another margarita and I might curl up on this couch and go to sleep. Not sure how management feels about napping patrons.

If they don't want to encourage us, they shouldn't make the seats so comfortable. I lose the fight against yawning.

"Wake up!" Sage jabs her finger between my ribs.

"Let me sleep. Maybe I'll wake up and this will all be a dream . . . a horrible, depressing, sad sack of a dream." I squirm away from her and snuggle a pillow.

"This is a good thing." Sage removes my cuddly cushion. "Neil's an iceberg. Innocent looking on the surface, but a whole other story down below. Icebergs are best admired from afar."

I don't think she's ever been a big fan of my ex-boyfriend. Too safe, too boring. Too predictable. Easy for her to say given she's with Lee, a South African rugby god with a heart as big and kind as his . . . feet.

"Without Neil's share of the bills, I can't live on my own based on my massage income from the spa. Even with the crazy tips, Aspen's real estate is out of reach. I'm looking at rentals with multiple roommates down valley. One place had bunk beds. Like camp." I groan and try to suck the last drops of tequila from the ice cubes in my glass.

"Do you want to be a massage therapist forever?" Mara asks.

"No," I answer without a second's hesitation. "I'm good with my hands and when you move to paradise, you do whatever it takes to stay."

Unless you're Neil. My ex, who bailed on me and our five-year relationship at the end of the ski season. His "it's over speech" made him sound like the boring, number-crunching, middle-aged asshole he's probably going to grow up to be.

Mae and Sage both snort. Mara, who moved here earlier this year and doesn't really get our humor, blinks her wide eyes at me.

I shake my head. "Don't make that dirty. I'm not that desperate. My massages don't have happy endings."

"I think a lack of orgasms in your life might be part of your problem." Smirking, Mae rolls her long, dark hair into a loose twist down her back. "There's plenty of men around here who would volunteer. A whole squad of eager and overly sexed, testosterone filled rugby players."

Sure, I could hook up with one of the local rugby players, but diving into the shallow end of the dating pool has disaster written all over it. I'd need a head injury to agree to have sex with one of those guys. Landon's like a ski parka with old lift passes still attached. Yes, we all know where he's been. He's dated half the women at this table. No, thanks.

"Easley's had a crush on you for a while," Sage volunteers.

Tall and flirty, Easley is nice enough, but in a big brother kind of way. "I'm sure some women out there love hairy men."

"The only fur I like is on animals." Mara laughs and waves over the waiter. "I've shaved enough cat balls, I never want to have to do it for a man."

"That's way more information about Jesse's sack than I ever needed." Mae finishes the last of the pitcher. "I could never be a veterinarian. Or a waxer."

I sigh. "I've seen way too many hairy backs during massages. Sometimes it's a complete surprise based on how a guy looks with his clothes on."

Simultaneously, we all shudder.

I continue. "Reality is Aspen's a small town. Not a lot of prospects for settling down."

Mae's mouth purses like she's sucked on a lime. "That's a horrible expression. Settle. Down. Nothing positive about those two words."

Sage gives me a sympathetic smile. "Maybe a summer fling could be good. There's enough influx of seasonal employees in the restaurants, tours, and outdoor sports outfitters to provide temporary options." I love Sage's optimism. "No reason you need to find Mr. Right."

Mae agrees. "Mr. Right Now should be your goal. And we can start tomorrow night at the rodeo."

"Yee haw!" Maybe someday I'll be able to believe Neil did me a favor.

Nursing my post margarita headache the next morning, I drag my sorry self and a tumbler of iced coffee out to my soon-to-be former condo's small balcony. My hat and oversized sunnies shade my eyes from the glare of the summer sun. With a sigh, I troll the rental listings on my phone. I have another month to find a place before my lease is up and I'm homeless. This afternoon I have three massage clients. Tomorrow two. It's June and the summer season is off to a slow start. At this rate, I'll have blown through my small savings by ski season. If I last that long.

This is not how I planned my year. Or my life.

Three things I knew for certain six months ago:

I was pretty sure my college boyfriend was going to become my husband someday.

We'd spend our lives together living in the mountains of Colorado.

I was definitely living the life I'd dreamed about as a teenager in the suburbs of Chicago.

Too bad it all fell apart.

Boyfriend decided to move back to "the real world" as he put it and be a "real adult" in Chicago. The air quotes and implied middle fingers are mine.

A few ski seasons and summers bumming around Aspen were enough for him. As if location and job, not age, define us as adults. Pretty sure Colorado still counts as being part of the real world, even if we have legalized pot. It's not like there are dragons and fairies flying around.

All Neil's "realness" kind of ruins the second and third things on my dream life list. The *we* is now an *I*. As in single, alone, and facing down thirty in four years.

Oh no. Now I'm having a quarter life crisis.

Add cliché to my list of what my life is now.

I'm probably going to end up a cautionary tale. Younger generations of idealistic women will whisper the name Zoe with a sad nod and downcast eyes.

At least Neil paid his share for the last two months. Out of the goodness of his bank account. Because the man wants his security deposit back. He'll do anything to avoid a financial penalty or heaven forbid, negative credit.

TWO

ZOE

I WILL NEVER look at a man in jeans the same way ever again.

Or boots. There's something so strong and tough about a pair of scuffed boots. Like he's been out doing manly things all day. Riding horses and kicking ass.

Who knew men's footwear could be hot? I didn't.

I'm okay admitting when I'm wrong.

And I've been wrong about cowboys.

Belt bling might be my new favorite thing. A beacon, a lighthouse showing me the way through the darkness of the post-break up blues.

Bigger than is polite for regular society, but not as obnoxious as a pro wrestling championship belt, the rodeo buckle is perfect.

I feel like Goldilocks when she stumbled upon the bears' house.

Not too big, not too small. Just right.

Or maybe it's the men behind the buckle.

Broad shoulders. Narrow waist. Biceps that can only be described as bulging.

Speaking of bulges, the beacon of the buckle definitely draws my eyes to the obvious selling point for a pair of Wranglers.

I'm not saying every man here is the stuff of fantasy, but there's enough eye candy to keep my interest.

I wonder if women follow the rodeos like patchouli-scented hippie chicks trail behind Phish.

And where do I sign up for this adventure? I can give massages to earn my way. My Mini Cooper might be able to tow a tiny camper.

Yes, I'm thinking about going on the road and towing a bed behind me.

My hormones have taken over.

I've clearly lost my mind.

Over some shiny brass with a bronco carved into it. I'm pretty sure it's a bronco. I haven't had the chance to examine one up close. Yet. This needs to be remedied as soon as this sexy horse and pony show is over.

Goals are important for a fulfilling life. I know this because the daily self-affirmations calendar Sage gave me reminds me. Every single day.

Another thing I've decided is the combined scent of leather and horse should be bottled. Add in some manly musk, and women would buy the shit out of it for the men in their lives.

Eau du cowboy.

Why hasn't anyone thought of this yet? There used to be the Marlboro Man, a cigarette smoking cowboy of the twentieth century. Who wants a man to smell like smoke? Especially when sage and leather exist? Throw in some sandalwood, and I'll hand over my panties.

This is what I imagine young Robert Redford smelled like. Now I get why my grandmother was obsessed with him and Paul Newman.

I can see a day filled with old Westerns on Netflix in my future.

"You have a glazed look, and is that drool?" Sage's finger

jabs near the corner of my mouth. "I can see the lust vibrating off of you. And a vibrator in your future."

After swatting away her finger and knowing I'm blushing from her last comment, I rub the knuckle of my index finger around my mouth. "There's no drool."

"You've got it ba-ad," Sage singsongs.

"So bad. Have you never seen a man on a horse before?" Mae joins in the taunting.

"Chicago police has a mounted unit. Evidently, they don't count." I focus my attention on the pen full of cowboys.

"Not even close to being the same thing." Mara looks a little flushed and glassy-eyed herself. "I doubt those horses buck and try to throw off the cops."

"I'm going to admit something I never thought I'd say or even think."

Holding their breath, the three of them wait for my declaration.

"I might have a thing for chaps." I tilt my head in the direction of a row of cowboys standing on the metal fence near the bulls. "It's a gift that keeps on giving. Front, back, and sides."

"I'd like the one on the end. Front, back, and sideways." Mae openly points at the dark-haired guy straddling the top rail.

I shove her hand down. "Don't be obvious."

Mae sticks her tongue out at me. "Okay, Zoe. I'm not the one who was shouting and moaning loudly when the one with the black hat was rolling his hips on the bronco. I think those kids behind us are going to have a lot of questions for mommy when they get home tonight."

I roll my eyes. "Not my fault if they don't know basic anatomy. I had no idea bull testicles were so huge."

Mara snorts. "Why do all our conversations end up being about animal balls? I get enough of them at work, please and thank you very much."

"I'd rather talk about making the suggestion of a cowboy scramble. Instead of letting a gaggle of sticky-fingered children loose on the dirt to grab a ribbon off the ears of those poor baby cows, they should let us have the chance." My idea is brilliant.

"Sweetie, you wouldn't stand a chance of grabbing some chaps against some of these cougars." Sage pats my arm. "We may be younger and faster, but they want it more."

She's right. I study the group of ladies sitting to our left. Bedecked and bejeweled in outfits that cost more than I could afford in rent, they're perfectly polished specimens of women. From their glossy yet wavy hair to their barre class sculpted arms, they could easily take down someone like me with a flick of their slightly pointed, almond-shaped nails.

I might be taller than most of them, but their lower center of gravity works in their favor. In my holey-kneed jeans and white T-shirt with gold sparkle 'Merica on the front, I'm definitely out of my league. At least my straw hat, a gift from Sage, is on point.

"Okay, bad idea. New idea: do you think we could volunteer for roping practice? Because damn if the way they lasso and tie-up those little calves isn't sexy." I'm definitely thinking of the multi-tasking and hand-eye coordination involved in riding a horse, swinging a rope, and catching a moving animal. Those seem like solid transferable skills.

"Someone get a bucket of water." Sage grins.

"Forget the bucket. We need a fire hose." Mara fans her hands at me. "Girl's on fire."

"Wasn't it the three of you who schooled me last night about moving on, having a summer fling?" Crossing my arms, I pretend to pout.

"True, but mostly that was the tequila talking." Mae pushes her palms toward me in the universal sign of "slow down, crazy."

After the rodeo ends, we loiter in the stands, waiting for the crowd of tourists and families to disperse.

A souvenir booth near the entrance catches my attention as we make our way out of the grandstand. They sell posters of the cowboys. Not since my tween heart pitter-pattered over my first crush have I had the urge to hang a poster of a cute boy in my room. I stumble and miss a step as I crane my neck, trying to see if the cowboy in the black hat has a poster.

My balance isn't helped by Sage, who slaps my back and squeals. "Why didn't I think of this? Stan and I are leaving for South Africa in a couple of weeks. You can dog sit for us and stay in my condo for all of July."

Barely listening because I'm still in a daze over the hot cowboys, I absently nod. "Sure. I like dogs."

A hand waves in front of my face. "Earth to Zoe."

I bat Mara's hand away. "What? I said I like them."

"She's in a cowboy stupor." Mara snaps her fingers close to my nose. "Snap out of it."

"I see no problem." I blink away the image of tight jeans and straw hats. With a shaky exhale, I glance longingly toward the horse trailers on the other side of the lot. "I feel like I've found out Santa, the Easter Bunny, and the Tooth Fairy are all real. And everyone's been keeping it a secret from me."

"They're just men who ride horses. And smell like horses." Mara wrinkles her nose.

"What's up with you and horses?" Mae asks.

"Classic story of a girl who fell off a horse and never got back on. I'm more of a unicorn fan."

"Maybe we should take riding lessons," I half-jokingly suggest.

Mara's big eyes grow even wider as she stares at me like I've just declared we go swimming with sharks.

"Come on, it'll be good for you. If I'm lucky the instructor might even be hot." I give her a thumb's up.

"Girl, you have a major case of the hornies. I say we go down to Woody Creek and see if you can find something nice and long to scratch your itch." Mae holds her hands about a foot apart and raises her eyebrows.

My eye catches on movement by the trailers before I can respond to her. "Do you think we're allowed to mingle with the talent after the show?"

"I don't think there's a VIP area or bouncers for a rodeo." Sage begins pulling me in the direction of the horses.

THREE

ZOE

"HELLO, DARLIN', CAN I help you?" tall, rough, and handsome drawls at me as I stand a few feet away, openly gawking at him. He's next to the horse he used for the roping competition. The beautiful brown and white Paint.

I want to pet your buckle.

I clear my throat and adjust my hat. "I . . . um, I . . ."

"Can we pet your horse?" Sage not so gently pushes me forward.

"She wants to pet more than the horse," Mae interjects loud enough for all of us to hear her, including the cowboy.

"She's kidding. Can I touch it?" My hand reaches out in his general direction of its own volition. I'm no longer in control of my body parts and I sound like the biggest pervert. "I mean your horse."

"Cisco?" He gives me a slow, lazy grin. Like no one has ever offered to pet his pony before.

I nod.

"Figures. He gets all the beautiful ladies. Here, you can feed him an apple." His warm eyes sparkle with genuine amusement as he pulls off a glove to reach into a bucket.

Instead of just handing me the apple, he lifts my hand and carefully places it on my palm, gently extending my fingers away from the fruit. "Don't feed him any fingers. Doc says he needs to cut down."

I'm only half listening because the scrape of his calloused hands over my skin creates a humming in my ears. "Okay. No fingers. Got it."

Cisco whinnies and stomps one of his front feet, impatient for his treat. Extending his neck, he opens his mouth, revealing huge teeth. I need my hands and fingers to work. This is a terrible idea. *How am I supposed to give massages if I only have stumps?*

I shift my hand a few inches out of reach, away from his mouth.

"Not fair to tease him. No reason to be shy." Cowboy cups my hand and moves it forward, making sure my palm is flat. A soft whisper of whiskers and velvet brush my skin when Cisco takes the apple.

I exhale an unsteady breath.

"Not used to being around horses?" Belt Buckle, or BB for short, gives me a knowing smirk.

"It's been a while." Like twenty-six years.

"If you want to get back on the horse, there's some good trail rides around here with amazing views. Pretty incredible with the right company. I know a place you can rent a horse for the day."

I think he just asked me out on a horse date.

The problem is I've never ridden a horse. First time on a horse with a man like him is a one-way ticket to Disaster Town.

"Oh, that's okay. I'm sure you're busy with rodeoing." Is that even a verb? It is now. I keep talking and hope it's a real word that people who aren't afraid of horses toss around. "Life on the circuit must be pretty crazy."

He gives me a shrug and goes back to stripping the gear off

his horse. His deft fingers work the leather and buckles with ease. Manual dexterity is an underrated attribute on dating sites. Intelligence, kindness, humor, and the ability to perform detailed work with hands, and other body parts, a must.

I'm still mentally reworking my requirements for all future potential boyfriends when it occurs to me I've just rejected him.

"I mean I'd love to go riding. With you. Next time you pass through these parts." Great, now I sound like I'm acting in a cheesy Western movie. At least I haven't called him partner. Yet.

Something I say makes him frown. "I'm going to be tied up with competitions. July's pretty insane for me."

"No problem. I didn't think you meant we'd go together." Not at all.

He studies me, his dark eyes reflecting the lights around the grandstand. "I could set you and your friends up, if you want to go."

"Please no," Mara says, backing away like he's going to toss her on Cisco's back right here and now.

Full of questions, Cowboy's dark eyes flash to me.

"She's what happens when you don't get right back on the horse," I explain.

He nods with understanding. "Only takes one bad fall."

Mara's shoulders droop with relief. "I love all animals, but I'm not a fan of riding them. This might be why I have cats."

He laughs. "Even if you can manage to get the saddles on, the little bastards would totally refuse to take the bit."

Mara's hazel eyes shine as she laughs. "Now I have to get cowboy hats for Fred and George."

Mae sighs. "Okay, crazy cat lady, let's not scare off the nice man while we're trying to make a good first impression for Zoe."

She means well, but her words douse the conversation in silence.

Thankfully, Sage ignores Mae and Mara, and smiles at BB. "We won't keep you. Congratulations on the win tonight."

While speaking, she's gently shepherding me away from Cisco. Before it's too late, I brush my hand down his strong, velvet soft neck.

BB dips the front of his hat. "Enjoy your evening, ladies."

He's polite and aloof, but when I turn back to get one last look, he's still watching me.

With a wink and that slow, sleepy smile, he removes his hat and executes a bow. Kind of like a western Mr. Darcy.

"Keep moving," Sage commands from my side. "Walking away is the most interesting thing you can do tonight."

"Huh?" Mae asks. "I thought the plan was to ride a cowboy to chase away her blues?"

"Not that cowboy." Sage links our arms and pats my hand. "Trust me."

"I saw the bulge in his jeans. He's packin'. What more does she need from cowboy man candy?" Mae's slowly following a few steps behind us.

"I'm not talking about what's in his pants. He didn't smear on the charm thick like a big dollop of butter on some hot cornbread."

"Mmm." I'm practically drooling. "Now I'm hungry."

"Me too," Mara says. "You think anything's still open besides pizza?"

"I could eat. We could go to the Stonebridge Inn and get bar snacks." Mae joins the push for food.

"I've lost you all." Sage laughs at our moaning. "Let's go get food and maybe you'll eventually let me finish my point."

"Tell me now, wise one," I whine and make puppy eyes at her.

"BB practically asked you out on a daytime date. He didn't suggest you join him and the rest of the ruffians for drinks tonight."

"Of course." I nod as understanding hits me. "He wasn't interested. I get it. Thanks for saving me from even more awkwardness."

The realization stings. For the first time in months, maybe even years, the thrill of potential hot sex started to bubble up. My body reacted on a primal level and obviously overshadowed the signals he was sending—the neon flashing "no" above his head clear to everyone but me.

"Stop. Just stop right there." Mae's voice holds annoyance and disappointment.

"You sound hangry," Mara whispers.

"I ate enough ribs for two, I'm not hungry. Just annoyed."

We've all stopped walking outside the main entrance. We're now the kind of people who get off an escalator and stop right at the bottom, forcing everyone else to navigate around us. Feels like we're about to create a scene.

I watch enough reality shows to know that a girls' night can turn into a cat fight in less time than it takes to do a shot.

"Keep it moving, ladies," I beg. "If we hurry, we can catch the first shuttle."

That gets my friends to speed up their meandering. Around here, we take the free shuttles when we go out drinking. Cheaper than an Uber and safer than hitting an elk after rosé all day.

It's a short ride up the winding road to the Stonebridge.

Snowmass doesn't really have a downtown center like Aspen. Instead there are two shopping areas that anchor the resort village. The open air mall with its shops, restaurants, and sports equipment rentals, is surrounded by condos, hotels, and on one side, the ski runs.

Unlike most of the rest of the world, places around here shut down for the slow months. Like families with kids who operate their lives around the school calendar, everyone who lives year-round in these mountain towns adjusts to life during the off season.

Sometimes I compare it to the forced naps we had to take in preschool. Didn't matter if you were jammin' out to Elmo and drawing a masterpiece, time for mandatory rest.

At first I thought it was weird. Sure, in Chicago we have four seasons, each with its own character. But unless there's a huge lake effect blizzard, the city doesn't shut down. Now I love the quiet times.

Not Neil. He didn't understand why he couldn't get sushi or steak at his favorite places seven nights a week. To some, like Neil, it didn't matter if he was the only person in the place. Probably made him feel special.

Wonderful.

Now he's crept into my head again and ruined my happy bubble.

"I think I might go home and crash." I'm already thinking about what Netflix show I can stream.

"No, you're not," Mae declares.

Damn she's pushy.

"Don't be discouraged about the cowboy." Sage leans around Mara to meet my eyes. "Like I was saying before. It's a good thing he wasn't trying to get in your pants tonight. You don't need to have sex with a random guy."

"She doesn't?" From my left, Mae tilts forward to stare at Sage. "Says who?"

"Quit interrupting and I'll tell you." Sage narrows her eyes, making sure we're all going to keep quiet. I imagine her giving the same look to her young dance students. Don't let the rainbow unicorn hair fool anyone, she's tough. "I think you need a guy friend who can help restore your faith in the male species."

"Like Lee?" I ask.

"Exactly. Not all men are spineless dickheads."

"Anyone else picturing eels right now?" Mara silently gags. "Just me?"

"Not hungry anymore." Mae leans back.

Sage ignores them and continues. "Find a guy you can be friends with. No expectations, no pressure."

"Preferably someone with terrible pheromones and halitosis. Back and shoulder hair might help too," Mara suggests. "It also might be helpful if you imagine them as an eel."

"Stop. No more mention of eels," Mae grumbles.

"I have guy friends. Lee and Jesse. Even Easley."

"The first two count, but they're our boyfriends. It would be weird if you start hanging out with them all the time without us," Mara says.

"Easley has the gorilla arms, so he qualifies." Mae doesn't look sure if this is a good thing or not.

"But with Easley usually comes Landon," Sage says, and we all frown.

"Definitely a negative." I make an *x* with my index fingers.

"Jesse knows everyone from ski patrol and construction. I'm sure he has a half-decent friend you can hang out with," Mara offers with a smile.

"What happened to a summer fling?" I ask, feeling more and more like a social experiment.

"If you have an itch, scratch it yourself?" Mae suggests, but clearly doubts this is a good thing. "I'm still on Team Fling. If anyone is asking."

"Me too," I say, softly. "You can't take a girl to the rodeo, show her all those men in their Wranglers, then tell her to look but not touch. You're all a bunch of mean girls."

"At least your sex drive isn't completely dead." Mae pats my shoulder. "I'd say the evening has been a success for that discovery alone."

Great. Now that things are zinging and pinging, I'm going home alone. I don't want to play it safe anymore. I want to be wild and daring, the kind of woman who doesn't care what society thinks of her choices. I want to live dangerously and not look back in another five years full of regret.

FOUR

JUSTIN

TONIGHT IN SNOWMASS, I'm too close to home to not be obsessed with sleeping in my own bed. A mattress instead of a bed roll sounds like heaven. It's been two weeks since I've woken up in my own place. That's about as long as I can stand.

A few of the younger bucks on the tour gather near their pickups, making plans for tonight's drinking and womanizing. Dusty, who earned the name for always ending up in the dirt when riding the broncos, waves me over.

"You joining us, old man?" He grins, loving to give me shit.

I give it right back to him with a grin of my own. "You inviting me because you need someone to buy you beer?"

"Turned twenty-one two weeks ago. You were at my party."

"Surprised you remember anything about that night." Poor kid vomited in his hat outside a bar in Cheyenne. Waste of a good Stetson, but most of us have done it at some point. A rodeo circuit rite of passage.

"You coming?" he asks.

"Heading home tonight. I've got a few days off and need to get some work done on the ranch." Not sure why I'm explaining all this to him. All the young guys care about is their ranking, their horses, women, and booze. The order of importance changes depending on the time of day.

If I ever was like that, I'm not anymore. Yeah, I'm only a few years older, but my focus has changed.

"Catch up with you in a few days. Maybe practice staying on the bronco instead of flopping around like a dying trout."

I accept the middle finger Dusty gives me and return it with a grin.

"Ready to go home?" I ask Cisco.

I swear he nods when he shakes his mane.

The darkening sky still holds a hint of blue as I ready Cisco for the trailer. Not sure if he can smell the familiar scents in the air, but when we compete in Snowmass, somehow, he knows he'll be sleeping in his own paddock with his horse buddies tonight. He flicks his tail and nuzzles my shoulder like he's telling me to hurry up so we can go home. My favorite roping horse, Cisco and I are kindred spirits.

"We'll get there. Stomping your feet won't speed up the process. You got a pretty girl to give you an apple. Stop complaining. You're doing better with the ladies lately than I am."

It's the truth.

A beautiful brunette with the prettiest deep brown eyes I'd ever seen came over to us after the show. Even with her group of friends egging her on, she seemed shy. Reluctant even. I tried to ask her to go riding with me, but she shot me down.

It's entirely possible she lost a bet and had to talk to a cowboy tonight. Wouldn't be the first time, but I can't say I'm not disappointed.

Rarely do the women who hang around rodeos interest me. I wish they did. Life would be simpler and I'd get laid more.

Shockingly, life on the Western State Rodeo Circuit isn't as glamorous as it sounds. Two to three shows a week in different towns means when I'm not riding, I'm driving. Or sleeping.

Sometimes I manage to eat and hang out with friends.

No, I don't fuck a different woman after every rodeo. Although I could.

And it's not to say that some of these guys don't. Hell, they're doing this not for the fame, money, or buckle bragging rights. They're in it for the women.

Missing a tooth? Tell her it got kicked out by a bronco.

Weird ass broken nose? Busted by a bull.

Cut lip? Let them wonder if it's from a bar fight or a horse.

The less we share, the bigger the mystery, and the fantasy.

Some of the women eat that shit up for breakfast, lunch, and dinner. At least they would if we stuck around long enough for more than a few beers and a night together.

Not that I'm judging the women. As long as they're being treated right, getting off, and then having something to brag about to their friends, more power to them. Hope the memory keeps them warm at night. Because Cowboy Joe won't be there to snuggle them.

There's a reason some men are still drawn to this life. We're restless spirits. Nothing kills us quicker than forcing us into a mundane routine, stuck in the same place, and caged by four walls. You want to break a cowboy? Force him to settle down.

The rodeo season's short. A couple of months in summer. We perform and compete in front of audiences in towns where city folk go for a taste of the mythical west. Hell, some of them probably pronounce rodeo like the drive in Beverly Hills. Honey, this ain't no ro-day-o, and I'm not wearing these chaps so you'll focus on my junk.

Don't confuse us with a Vegas male revue. For the most part, we keep our pants on around here. At least during competitions.

After every show, women gather near the riders like Black Friday shoppers. Sometimes there's even jostling and elbows being thrown to get the opportunity to chat with one of us. It'd be pretty amusing if it weren't the same thing every damn night.

Sweaty, smelling like horse or bull, tired but hopped up on adrenaline, we're pretty feral. Yet the women flock to us like hungry gulls and we're the lone french fry on the beach.

Most nights I have a beer and then find a place to set up my tent. Sure, I could stay in one of the local motels with the bed bugs and enough bodily fluids sprinkled around to fill a crime lab, but I prefer to keep my own company.

If I can sleep with a view of the stars, even better.

This might be one of the reasons I'm never interested in a random hookup. I'd probably get pretty strange looks if I invited a woman back to my tent.

Pretty sure the cowboy fantasy would end right then and there.

Then again, maybe not.

One thing I've learned about women is when they set their mind to something, it takes more than a little convincing them to get them to shift. Same's true with horses.

Both have long memories about real or perceived slights.

FIVE

ZOE

FOR THE LAST time ever, I stand in the living room of the apartment I shared with Neil.

Traffic and music from outside filter in through the closed windows. My footsteps echo in the empty space. Boring white walls show no sign we ever lived here.

When I met Neil, I was a fine arts major. I've always known I wanted to make beautiful things and accepted I'll never be rich. In a crisp blue button-down and flat front khakis, Neil promised stability and a solid future with his business major. He was the planner to my free spirit. The calendar to my winging everything.

In school, I spent long nights in the ceramics studio, managing my kilns while Neil slept soundly, getting his eight hours of brain rest every night.

He went for an MBA and I got an MFA. What a difference one letter makes.

For years, I thought he was the ying to my yang. The gravity for my moon. It's easy to ignore the lack in common when the future is neatly outlined in a spreadsheet and matching Roth IRAs.

With a sigh, I lock the door of our former life, leaving that future behind me.

I stand next to my car trying to figure out if I should cry.

Just in case, I put on my oversized sunglasses for dramatic flair. That's what Neil would say, how us artsy types have a flair for the dramatic. No matter if clay and theater have zero to do with each other, the "arts" are all the same: full of too much emotion.

Part of me wants to create a spectacle to piss him off, even if he's thousands of miles away. Force some sort of reaction from steadfast, stoic, there's-a-rational-answer-for-everything Neil Chase.

For one fantastic moment, I imagine myself lighting a cigarette and walking away as the condo complex burns behind me. Like *Heathers*.

Of course I'd only be hurting myself. And the innocent neighbors who probably wouldn't appreciate me destroying everything they own. At least in jail I'd get room and board. Probably some sort of art room to rehabilitate me and my evil, pyromaniac ways.

This is who I am now. Contemplating the benefits of being locked up versus single and struggling.

I need to get out of here. Giving the middle finger to the closed door of my old life, I fail to feel any satisfaction.

A good sobfest sounds like the perfect way to mark this moment. And cake. I'm going to need some cake, too. If it's appropriate for funerals as well as weddings, then breakup cake should be a thing. Maybe an ice cream cake. With sprinkles. Covered in salted caramel. Or regular caramel with the added salt from my tears.

This needs to happen.

Ignoring the dark sky threatening rain, I open the sunroof on my racing green Mini Countryman.

Rain today would be too much of a cliché.

Like a sad girl eating her feelings, and weight, in sugary carbs.

Delicious cake, here I come.

Large circles of rain splat against my windshield before I reach the rotary into Aspen. Of course. Because this is my life.

As the drops turn into a downpour, I press the button to close the roof.

Nothing happens.

Except rain splashing down on me and everything else inside the car. I press and hold the button, hoping to force it to reboot itself like a computer or phone. Cars should be the same way.

Should, but aren't.

My windshield wipers swish away the water on the glass, but do nothing to help me. Blindly, I reach behind me in the backseat for a hat.

I touch something stiff and pull a straw hat between the seats. It's from the rodeo a couple of weeks ago. The wide brim creates an umbrella for my head. I can see why cowboys love these.

The rain continues as I drive to Clark's and the promise of breakup cake. If I can't close the roof, I'll also have to get something to cover the opening so my car doesn't become a fish tank. A black garbage bag will work, and be the least classiest thing to ever be seen on the same streets where the Kardashians have hung out.

My luck improves when I find a spot right in front of the market. With my new favorite hat on, I only look like a partially drowned cat, one with great taste in accessories.

After finding a towel in the backseat—which is kind of like the car version of Mary Poppins' bag—I toss it over the dashboard to protect it from getting soaked. Even I know electrical systems and water don't mix.

I get a few odd stares as I leave the car with the roof open. What's wet is wet. To prove my point, I step in a large puddle next to my door.

Standing under the store's awning, a woman holding a pale pink Birkin bag points at my car. "Your roof's open. It's raining."

Tilting my head back, I let rain hit my face. "Huh, I hadn't noticed. Thanks."

Water drips from my bare arms while she remains perfectly dry and fresh. I'm tempted to stand close to her and shake like a dog. I'd probably get sued for getting her bag wet. Understandable because it costs about the same as I paid for the used Mini.

Inside, my shoes squeak on the sparkling clean floor. Or maybe it's my feet making the squishing sounds inside my sneakers with each step. Either way, the stares continue.

I should probably tell someone to set out the Caution Wet Floor sign in the aisles where I walk. When it's my turn to pay, I set my five items on the belt and try to see them from someone else's perspective.

Black garbage bag. Box cutter. Duct tape. Cake. Prosecco.

Clearly, I'm celebrating burying a body.

Or kidnapping someone for their birthday, but taking it to the extreme. Because the only triple chocolate cake available cheerfully wishes a happy birthday in bright blue lettering. I plan to scrape off the words as soon as I get home.

Oh wait, I don't have a home.

I can eat my cake in my wet car with the plastic roof.

Ain't nobody who can rock a hot mess like this girl.

"Looks like you're planning a fun evening," a male voice comments behind me in line.

I give a light "ha ha" without turning around to acknowledge that he spoke, because I have zero desire to engage with some random man about my purchases. I don't care what he has to say. The quicker I can get out of here, the sooner I can save my car, and my dignity.

"You going to eat that cake with someone special?" he continues like we're having a conversation. I can't believe he's hitting on me when I look like a half-drowned country mouse.

I step forward to pay the cashier and catch a familiar face out of the corner of my eye.

"Oh." Landon. Sage's ex. Rugby player. Clueless flirt. Generally annoying human.

"Hi, yourself." He gives me a sly smirk. "Interesting night planned?"

"Wouldn't you like to know?" I try to mimic his expression like we're playing the mirror game. I'm not sure I master the extra slime he manages to add to his smile.

"Is that an offer? Because I admit I'm more than curious. I never figured you for a criminal. Or kinky." He says the last word loud enough to catch the cashier's attention along with two people in the next line.

"We all have a dark side." I pull out my card to pay.

"No one should spend their birthday alone. Invite me over and I'll help you celebrate." He steps closer and into my space.

He has to be kidding. Has to, but isn't.

"Never said it's my birthday. In fact, I haven't told you anything about my plans. But thanks for assuming I'm a loser."

I pay and say thank you to the cashier, trying to ignore Landon's presence.

"See you around soon," he shouts behind me as I leave the store. "Now that you're single, we should hang out more."

Great. Guess word of the breakup has spread to the rugby club. They'll be on me like vultures with fresh roadkill. It's not a pretty image for good reason.

For years I've watched the players of the Pitkin Country Rugby Club flirt and sleep their way through this town. I suffered through Sage's relationship with Landon. Why would I ever want to repeat her mistake?

The rain has eased to a half-hearted sprinkle.

I open the door and stand on the footboard to reach across the top. The bag covers the sunroof. I use the box cutter to make strips of the tape, praying it won't damage my paint.

Stretching to reach the far side of the roof, I hear male laughter behind me.

"Would've been happy to help you out, but feel like I should say thank you for the view."

I glance at Landon standing a few feet behind me. In my short cutoffs, I'm sure I'm giving him an eyeful.

"You're not welcome." After patting the tape in place, I hop down. "Aren't there some fresh tourists for you to sucker, I mean, seduce?"

"Got a match tomorrow. You should come and cheer for me." He lowers his mirrored Ray-Bans so he can wink at me.

His move is so over the top I snort out a laugh. I'm laughing at him, not with him, but it doesn't matter to a narcissist like Landon. He has my attention and that's all that matters.

Without another word, I sit down and close the door behind me. Turning on the engine, I realize I'm sitting in a puddle and now it feels like I've peed my pants.

This day keeps getting better.

I turn on the seat warmers, hoping it will dry out the leather and my shorts on the way home.

Pulling into Sage's driveway, I put the car in park. I glance up at the plastic bag ceiling. Unless we get a crazy thunderstorm, it'll hold until I can get down valley and fix the sunroof.

For giggles, I press the button again, just to make sure it's really broken.

Somewhere God laughs as the glass slides smoothly back into place.

SIX

ZOE

ONCE INSIDE, I set the cake and bag of crime supplies on the kitchen counter. Sage's condo is a twin to Lee's, right next door. The two of them have been living here with the dogs while they figure out what to do with his place. There's no point in having two separate units or blowing out the wall and trying to create one monster unit. Not when the two of them have ridiculous bank and can probably afford to buy a house around here.

This is one gift horse I'm not looking in the mouth. I'm incredibly lucky I get to live here, cost free, while I figure out my single life. No more plus one for me.

Time for cake.

I open the box and slide my pinky through the birthday greetings, smearing it into a colorful blur of messy lines and swirls.

Who needs a fork when you plan to eat the entire cake yourself?

I jab a finger into the soft ganache and sink into the moist cake and mousse filling before breaking off a chunk. I moan when the chocolate melts on my tongue.

"*Delishsush,*" I slur around a mouth full of heaven. My little piece isn't enough. I form a scoop with my hand and stuff a giant glob of deliciousness into my mouth, not caring I now have chocolate all over my fingertips and probably my face.

Standing at the counter, I eat cake and think about how I ended up here. A life stuffed into a few mismatched pieces of luggage and cardboard boxes. At least if I decide to become a buckle bunny and follow the rodeo, all the important stuff will fit in my tiny car.

Nell and Hunter, my furry responsibilities for the next month, are playing tug by the couch. It's completely adorable how they play together. This is the easiest gig ever. About a year old, they're fluffy brown mixes of awesome.

Free rent, limited responsibilities, and a whole summer to play. Hello, teenage dream come true.

Nell growls and jerks the toy away from Hunter. She might be his sister, but she's the alpha in their relationship. Poor Hunter never wins.

Doesn't stop him from trying.

Thinking there's some life lesson in Hunter's optimism, I shove in another mouthful of cake. I happily chomp away until a flash of white dangling from Nell's mouth causes me to pause and set down my glob of cake.

"Drop it." I lick my fingers as I scramble to get to the living room before she can swallow what appears to be my one and only phone charger that still works.

Using her distraction as his big opportunity, Hunter snatches the cord out of her mouth and dashes around the living room in a victory lap.

"Hunter, drop it." I focus on him. He stares at me and tilts his head, probably wondering if he can take me in round two of the tug o'war.

I take a step toward him and something sharp bites into the bottom of my foot. Without looking, I can tell by the shape, it's the USB end of my cord.

"Fuck," I curse and dislodge the sad square from my instep.

Hunter drops the rest of the cord, his joy dimmed by the harsh tone of my voice. Fun time is over.

"It's okay," I tell him. "These things last about a month. Tops. Even when someone doesn't eat them."

His tail wags, hoping whatever made me mad has passed.

Sensing the new tension in the room, Nell bumps my leg with her nose.

Dogs chew on stuff. Fact.

Sometimes it's a toy, sometimes it's a shoe. Or throw pillow. Or a bra.

Sure it's naughty, but staying mad doesn't teach them to not chew on everything. It's all about managing impulse control and positive reinforcement of the behavior I want.

Giving Nell a scratch by her collar, a realization hits me.

I don't want to train a man. Or be trained to fit into a neat, sterile life full of meeting expectations and hitting milestones set by someone else.

Which is exactly what I did with Neil. His praise became my motivation. Pleasing him meant I was a good girlfriend, which equaled being a good person.

"Bullshit," I swear as I toss both ends of my charger into the trash. After washing the sticky frosting off my fingers, I pick up my cake box, grab a fork, and move to the couch.

I'm eating cake for dinner. And if there's any left, having it for breakfast, too.

In fact, if I want, I'm going to live off of cake. Cupcakes, coffee cake, Bundt cake, mini Bundt cakes, pound cake, and muffins. Because let's be honest, they're really cake, too . . . but without frosting.

Major life decision made, I settle into the cushions. With the cake balanced on my stomach, I turn on the television.

One hand holding my fork, I scroll to my streaming options. I'm all caught up on the *Great British Bake Off*. Sadly. Because what's better than watching people make cake while eating cake? Right now, in my life? Not much.

No Rom Coms or Nicholas Sparks' unhappily ever after sob stories. Horror? Don't need the nightmares. Drama? Hello, welcome to my life. Comedy? Eh. Sci-fi? Meh.

I need some strong women kicking ass. Or a fight of good versus evil. Maybe something with a cowboy.

Hmm. Western.

No one said all cowboys are off limits.

I wonder if there are any rodeo movies. I don't need an old black and white movie. Nor do I want something with white guys in brown makeup pretending they're "savage natives." *Ugh, no.*

Shaking my preconceived notions about Westerns is going to be tough.

I decide on *The Magnificent Seven* with Chris Pratt because he's my favorite Marvel hero. Because he's hot and funny. The perfect combination.

"Not so much tongue, Chris. Slow down and give a girl some time to warm up before you start licking her face." I'm stunned the man of my Hollywood fantasies is a terrible kisser. I really thought he'd be perfect in every single way.

"Dude, your breath could use a mint, too. Did you just eat a burger with onions?" I lift my hand to block his mouth from further attack. When my fingers stroke fur, my dream fades away and I open my eyes. Hunter's smiling white dog teeth grin back at me as he sweeps his soft tongue along my palm

"Ew." I wipe my other hand over my mouth. "Dog kisses."

Sadly, this is the most action I've had in months.

Stretching my arms over my head, I lean into Sage's super comfy couch. The cushions are probably stuffed with feathers from angel wings. Or naturally shed organic angora fur from pampered rabbits. Something ridiculously expensive and out of my price range.

In my horizontal position, I realize the cake box is tilted on its side, and I panic. Dogs can't have chocolate and this cake is chocolate held together with butter and sugar. *Shit. Crap.* I'm a terrible dog sitter. I scramble to find my phone while checking the box for evidence of paw-prints or tongue marks.

Unless I continued eating after I passed out in my sugar coma, it's clear someone besides me has helped themselves to some of the deliciousness.

There's no way I ate half a cake and wouldn't remember. *Is there?*

I inspect both dog's muzzles for chocolate and smell their breath for the telltale sweetness.

Neither gives me a definitive answer, so I call Mara.

"Hello?" her sleepy voice answers on the third ring. "Why are you calling me so late?"

"It's ten o'clock."

"Tomato, tomahto. What's up?"

"I think the dogs ate chocolate cake."

"Please tell me you didn't give them cupcakes." She yawns. "How much did they eat?"

"Swiss triple chocolate cake. And I'm not sure the amount because I was passed out in a sugar coma."

"Yum." Another yawn follows along with sounds of shuffling fabric. "It happens. How much did you eat?"

"I'm not sure. After the first few bites, it's all a haze."

"Did you slice it?"

Even though she can't see me, I feel my cheeks heat. "No. Listen, sometimes a woman needs cake. As a grown up, I'm allowed to eat a cake if I want. Without judgment or slices."

"I'm not judging. I'm trying to figure out how much the dogs ate. If they ate it."

"Hunter had some frosting on his nose and was licking my face when I woke up."

"I think they're okay given their weight and the type of chocolate. If you want, you can bring them over here and we'll induce vomiting. Or you can watch them overnight for symptoms."

"Let's avoid unnecessary vomit." I gag at the thought.

"They might throw up on their own. If they do, call me and bring them over. And next time, don't pass out with chocolate cake."

"Yes, Doctor."

This is my life now.

SEVEN

JUSTIN

I'M UP WITH the rooster this morning.

When I push back the curtains of my bedroom window, the faint purple-tinted light barely creates shadows among the tall lodgepole pines.

A glance at the clock on my nightstand confirms my fear.

It's not even six a.m. yet.

Shoot me. So much for sleeping in on my days off.

Or better yet, shoot the rooster.

Winner, winner, chicken dinner.

From my cabin, I can see the cock preening around the yard like he owns the place. The way he prances around and squawks reminds me of some of the cowboys I know. Dude ain't even the biggest cock in the yard.

If we're having a competition around here, I've got nothing to worry about. Never have.

Do guys compare? We can't help it.

Women say it doesn't matter, but the way their eyes light up when they see me naked for the first time says different.

Sounds like this makes me the cockiest bastard around. Maybe, but I don't need to fluff up my feathers to prove a damn thing.

My morning wood still heavy in my boxers, I meander my way into the bathroom. Even though she shot me down, or maybe because of it, the memory of beautiful deep brown eyes and pouty lips from the rodeo a couples weeks ago help me take care of business.

Sure some guys count their worth by the notches on their bedposts, the numbers in their phones, or the size of their buckles, but not me.

In the end, when we take our last breath, none of that bullshit will matter.

After a quick shower, I sweep my hand over my head, pressing the buzzed hairs down and then back up. When I was a kid, my grandmother would shave my head the day after school ended.

The woman grew up sheering sheep and knew her way around a pair of sheers. She'd leave me as bald as a kid with hair could possibly be, earning me the nickname Buzz.

Out of habit or nostalgia, I tend to keep the tradition. End of ski season, I break out the clippers and say good-bye to the long mess of brown waves. Easier and cooler when I'm out on the trails to have zero hair than be *that* guy who has a ponytail. Or a man bun.

Never. I'd have to punch myself in the face and I hate violence.

Ponytail cowboys only exist on the cover of my grandmother's romance novels. She gets older, but her fantasy cowboys never age. She's a saber tooth tiger compared to the younger cougars who show up at the rodeo.

Wearing only my boxer briefs, I set the kettle on the stove, then grind beans for coffee. When it comes to my morning brew, I'm more than particular. Even when I'm on the road or on a trail ride, I demand good coffee.

The sound of a triangle jangles the quiet morning.

Breakfast's ready in the communal dining room.

Slamming screen doors create a random drum beat around the ranch as everyone answers the call for grub.

Most of the bunkhouses are doubles, some are even quads, but I have a single. Living room in the front, small kitchenette against one wall, then a hallway with a simple bathroom and a bedroom dominated by a queen size bed in the back. Nothing fancy.

Just the way I like it.

Life is better when it's simple.

My grandfather sold his soul for this land.

To say I feel an obligation to keep this place going, to protect what they made with blisters and blood, is to underestimate the Garrison sense of home.

A few miles down the road, people spend millions on condos where they might spend a couple of weeks in a year.

The Easy Z ranch is the marrow in my bones.

I'll do everything I can to protect it, and my family's legacy.

After pulling on a pair of faded jeans I find tossed over the chair in the corner of my bedroom, I grab a white T-shirt half-folded on the top of the dresser. Uncertain if it's clean or not, I give it the sniff test. Good enough for this bunch of ya-hoos, I tug it over my head feeling a slight tinge in my shoulders from my rough dismount off a bull last night.

By the time I stuff my feet into a pair of worn work boots, I know I'll be scraping up the dregs of breakfast from the buffet. Around here it's not dog eat dog. More like a swarm of locusts, leaving nothing edible in their wake.

I zip my fly and tuck in the front of my T-shirt as I hop-walk back into the kitchen. After pouring my coffee into a stainless travel mug, I jog to the larger log building holding the dining hall and kitchen. Living on the ranch is a lot like living at summer camp. A camp only populated with half-wild men.

Sure enough, there's no bacon and a single, sad patty of sausage left in the meat tray of this morning's buffet. I manage to scoop enough eggs to fill the spoon from the dregs. Looks like I'm eating mostly hash browns and toast today. Who needs vegetables or color on their plate? Evidently no one around here.

Tammy, head cook, steps through the swinging door from the kitchen as I wait for the toaster to pop. Her cheeks are flushed and her curly gray hair is frizzier than normal.

Wiping her hands on her stained red gingham apron, she frowns at my mostly empty plate. "That all you're eating?"

"Morning to you, too. Got here late."

She sighs and stacks the empty containers. "Two eggs over easy, extra pepper, coming up."

"You don't have to—"

The swinging door tells me it doesn't matter what I say. I'm getting extra eggs.

In the time it takes for my toast to finish, Tammy returns carrying a plate with the two eggs as promised along with three slices of bacon.

"I'm not a growing boy anymore, T." I accept the plate, adding the other food to this one before buttering my dark toast. Just shy of burnt and exactly how I like it.

"You'll always be that scrawny kid to me." If she were closer, she'd probably pinch my cheek or waist like she used to do when I first arrived here as an angry teenager.

"If I keep gaining weight, Cisco's going to have a gripe with you."

"You spoil that horse. I keep sayin' you need a woman."

"When you gonna marry again, Tammy? It's about time you find a new husband."

Her lips tighten into a small ball and her eyes narrow. "You don't think three exes are enough for one woman?"

"Fourth time might be the charm," I tease.

"The first three were charmers. I've had enough charm to last me well into my old age."

I tip my chin down.

"You keep your mouth shut. I'm still in my prime."

I don't remind her she'll be sixty-five before I turn thirty in three years. Old enough to be my grandmother, she's taken on the role of a mother hen. Not only for me, but most of the guys who work around the ranch.

"Eat your food and keep your thoughts to yourself. Nobody wants cold eggs." Waving me away, she heads back into the kitchen.

"Look who turns up late and gets fancy eggs." Jeb jabs his fork at my plate when I join him at a rectangle table with a nicked and scarred top. "You flash Tammy your new buckle?"

I fake a chuckle. "She's not like the women you hang around. A little flash of brass doesn't charm her."

At least not anymore. Tammy's first two husbands were rodeo cowboys. When ex number two left her for a stripper he met in Reno, she stayed behind on the ranch. She's run the kitchen operation here for thirty years. Like the wide beams and pine tables, she's a fixture in the dining hall.

"All women need is to see me walking in with the hat and boots. They're practically in my lap even if I'm standing." Jeb leans back in his chair, full asshole smirk on his freckle dotted face. His nose peels a little from too much sun and his blond hair dips over the collar of his wrinkled red plaid shirt.

"Then what happens when they get a good look at your ugly mug in the light?" I dodge his attempt to flip my plate by lifting it and cradling it away from him.

"Not all of us can be pretty boys from California like you." His teasing holds an edge. It's too early for bullshit.

"What crawled into your boot and bit you this morning?" I

stab my egg with my bacon and scoop up some of the soft yolk.

Tammy always gets them just right. She deserves a raise. I know, I'm the one who oversees the ranch's operating expenses.

Knowing her, she'd tell me to give the money to someone who needs it more. She has a cabin of her own, a little garden, and can ride any time she wants. According to her, what does she need with money sitting in the bank?

I wish more people were like Tammy. Hell, I wish I were.

I'm trying.

Jeb's droning on about something. I catch a few words, but don't bother to listen to today's list of complaints as I eat my breakfast. Twenty-two and been here for four summers, he's too young to be this cynical.

"Well, you know what I always say." Finished eating, I wad up my napkin and toss it on my clean plate. "Don't like it here, you're welcome to try out another ranch. See how it suits you."

That shuts him up. "I'm not saying I want to quit the Easy Z. No way."

"Then maybe lay off the complaining and focus on what you can do to make things better." My tone is crankier than I mean it. "When you're in the horse business, you have to deal with shit."

"Okay, old man. Thanks for the wisdom." Jeb pushes himself away from the table. "I've got a group of ladies showing up here in an hour for a trail ride."

"First, I'm twenty-seven, not seventy-seven. Second, behave yourself." I finish my coffee and start thinking about today's to-do list.

"I'm here to show them a good time. And I always do." He gives me a proud smirk. "You may be the rodeo champ, but I'm keeping our customers happy and spreading the word about the ranch. You should pay me extra for the good PR."

I'd be worried about him harassing customers, but he always

has good reviews and we haven't had any complaints about inappropriate behavior. Yet.

"Do your job and maybe you'll get an extra s'more at the campfire."

"Cheap ass bastard," he mumbles, picking up his hat.

Like most guys around here, myself included, Jeb's all talk and no action. We put on a good show, but the truth of the matter is we live in a bunch of cabins in the mountains, working from dawn to dark. Doesn't leave a lot of room for too much mischief.

Depending on our mid-season review, we might need to reinstate the nighttime curfew. Nothing good ever happens around here after midnight. Nothing but trouble shows up at that time of night.

When my grandfather started the ranch, he had a strict nine o'clock curfew and expected everyone to show up for breakfast by five thirty. Said it kept the men honest.

He'd balk at how we run things around here now. Sometimes I think he haunts the place to keep an eye on us.

If anyone had the power to come back from the other side, it would be old Rex Garrison. I suppose when you make a deal with the devil, there are some perks.

After clearing the table, I decide to take a stroll around the property. Today's trail groups will be showing up soon and it's a good time to check out the crew as they prep for the day.

Sunlight peeks through the thin pines and aspens, casting the simple wood cabins in dappled light. I note some areas that need repair. Anything urgent will take priority this summer. Everything else can wait until things slow down in the off season this fall.

I greet a few customers and flash my friendly smile at the women openly ogling the guys as they tack up the horses. Western saddles are heavier than English, so there's plenty of bulging biceps action for the ladies to appreciate.

We keep older mares in the stable for the newbie riders. Slow and gentle with zero desire to gallop or run off, they're the perfect horse for tourists to have a Colorado horse experience. I compare them to those motorized scooters with the baskets at the big box stores. You'll get where you're going eventually, but not quick.

Letting Jeb and Luke take the lead, I loiter around the edge of the group. A tall brunette in a baseball cap and braids catches my attention. From the side, I'm certain it's the woman who fed Cisco the apple a couple of weeks ago at the rodeo. So convinced, I stroll over to her and tap her shoulder.

My lips curve into a happy smile at running in to her again. "Glad you're getting back on the horse."

Only it's not the same woman. While she's pretty, her blue eyes and narrow nose are not what I expected. Nor is the wide-eyed surprise. Or Botox filled forehead.

She slides her eyes down my torso and legs before a sultry grin forms on her glossy lips. "Well, I'd rather ride you. If the saddle fits."

Abort! Abort!

From my left, I hear Jeb's snort that he tries to pass off as a sneeze.

"Bless you," I say, loudly.

Distracted by glaring at him, I don't see the hand snaking around my side until I feel a pinch on my ass.

"Pardon me." I try to keep my voice neutral and resist the urge to rub my right cheek. With a smile plastered on my face, I take a step away from the client.

"Don't worry, I'm only teasing," she purrs. "I prefer bareback."

And with that, I'm out of here.

"Sorry, ma'am, but I won't be joining the ride today. You're in good company with Jeb and Luke. I'm sure they'll be happy to meet all your needs."

Cheesy innuendo or not, I know both of the guys can handle whatever she throws at them. Nothing we haven't seen or heard before.

"Happy trails!" I back away, keeping the smile on my face and my ass protected.

Sometimes I need to feel the uneven earth beneath my own feet. The idea of summer being relaxing and lazy is foreign to any of us around the ranch.

Between rodeos, trail rides, overnights, and riding lessons, the Easy Z buzzes with activity. Things won't quiet down until the last aspen leaf falls. Then we'll get a short break before winter season with the sleigh rides and snowmobile tours.

We do all of this to keep our land in the family.

Like a real estate agent going on about location, location, location, I know if we were to ever lose the ranch, we'd never have another chance to own acreage in these mountains again.

My ancient olive green pack along with a solo tent, bedroll and supplies leans against the cabin's wall, waiting patiently for our next adventure.

Screw it.

Missing two days of training isn't going to decrease my ranking. I'm already number one and my lead is steady. What will improve my mood is getting away from people demanding things from me.

I change out of my jeans into cargo shorts and stuff a change of clothes in the pack in case I fall in a stream or get caught in a storm. Wet socks are high on the list of things I can't stand

and the quickest way to get blisters on a hike.

Finding Tammy in the kitchen, prepping for lunch, I tell her I'm taking off for the back country beyond Maroon Bells.

"When you planning on being back? I need to know when to send out the search party for you." She opens the fridge and stacks several sandwiches, hard boiled eggs, and some peaches on her bent arm. "You pack any food? Real food, not that dehydrated crap?"

"You know the answer."

She shakes her head and sets her bounty on the stainless steel counter next to me. "I don't understand rich people. You could be eating filet and lobster every night, and you insist on torturing yourself with freeze dried disappointment."

"Who said I was rich?" I frown at her.

"Oh, psshaw. I've been around your family for too long to be called a fool."

"Psshaw? Watch your language." My mouth opens in fake outrage. I easily dodge the towel she snaps at my hip. "And physical assault? Here I was thinking we should give you a raise after your kindness this morning."

"What am I going to do with more money in the bank?" She crosses her arms in genuine annoyance. "Another thing I've learned from your family over the years is money only brings trouble. Got enough of that on my own."

With a laugh, I ask, "You think you can control the mayhem around here for a couple of days? I'll be back Monday morning."

"Don't you have to be in Crested Butte Monday evening for a rodeo?"

"I'll make it in plenty of time." Before she can stop me, I quickly lean down and kiss her cheek. Rarely does Tammy tolerate any affection or outward kindness.

"Shoo!"

"If anyone asks, you're in charge until Monday," I holler as the screen door slams behind me.

"Quit slammin' my doors!" Tammy yells from inside. "Next person who slams a door is gonna pay me a dollar."

EIGHT

ZOE

NEITHER HUNTER OR Nell get sick after the chocolate cake incident. A few days later I'm still apologizing for waking her up when I drop them off with Mara. Because I'm hiking to Crested Butte.

Yes, hiking.

Way too early for a Monday morning and my day off, I'm sitting in the passenger seat of Mae's ancient yellow VW bug, sounding like the sullen teenager I feel like. I'm also pretty sure I can see the road through the gaps of rust in the floor. Maybe walking would be safer than driving this tuna can of a car over a mountain pass.

"We're going to walk *over* the mountains to get to a place we can easily drive to? On roads? In my car with AC and a jammin' playlist? Why?" I'm whining. Probably due to the fact I'm awake and dressed before six in the morning. And I'm not coming home from a night out.

My phone started squawking at me before the sun had crested the mountain peaks. We're talking early enough to beat the birds to the earliest worms. Sounds like horrible motivation to me. A little gag at the thought of eating a worm forces my mouth open and I cough to clear my throat.

"What's in Crested Butte?" I sip the coffee she gave me as a peace offering.

"Life's not about the destination. It's a beautiful journey."

I jab my index finger into the fleshy part of her shoulder.

"Ouch!" She swerves into the oncoming lane for a second as she jerks her shoulder away. Her tone is harsh, but joking when she glares at me. "Don't use your super anatomy knowledge for evil."

I shrug. "It's too early for platitudes and clichés."

"Big words for someone who swears she's not awake yet."

The road to the start point winds past the Highlands ski area and twists through dense forests as we climb to the Maroon Bells.

A bend takes us into a grove of skinny pine trees dotted with small log cabins. Resting on two hand-hewn log posts, a rustic metal sign spans the narrow road.

"The Easy Z Ranch. Sounds like your rap name." Mae chuckles at her own joke.

"That's me. Easy Z. Right. Middle class white girl from the Chicago suburbs." I tuck my thumbs in my armpits and attempt to look tough.

"What are you doing? Please tell me you're not going to smell your fingers."

"What?" I jerk my hands away and sit on them. "No, I was being *gangsta*."

"About as gangster as the Disney Channel."

She's totally right. "I'm so glad my mother didn't push me into being a child actor. Dance, gymnastics, theater, art classes. I was well on my way to being precocious."

"Same, same, same, but throw in skiing and snowboarding. My dad swore I had the skills to be an Olympian."

"Seriously?"

"He wanted me to train for the trials."

"What happened?"

"A tale as old as these mountains. I rebelled. I discovered boys and the joy of pissing off my parents." Her voice is flat as she says all this like she's reciting off the dinner specials at work.

"You gave up a shot at the Olympics?"

"I wasn't *that* good. Around here we grow up on skis, starting as soon as we can walk and not face plant. I liked the speed and lack the fear gene. I'm fast." She shrugs off the conversation. "Someday I'll figure out what I want to do. No way am I going to wait tables forever."

"It must be strange to grow up in a place like this."

"Aspen's a small town. Like a lot of other small towns, you have the same kids in your class from kindergarten to graduation."

"With Hollywood celebrities and billionaires walking the streets."

"You kind of get immune to it. We were more excited about the X Games because we might know some of the athletes. Local kids making the big time."

"That's crazy. I didn't know anyone famous in Chicago. Does Sage count? She has a trust fund and her family does a lot of fundraisers. Or Lee? He's modeled." I shake my head at his unfortunate man bun phase.

As we follow the sweeping curves of the road, a few glimpses of the famous maroon peaks greet us, only to disappear around the next turn. Because it's still too early for humans, the ranger booth is empty when we arrive. Mae fills out the overnight parking pass and slips some money in the envelope.

"If we don't get the car tomorrow afternoon, they'll know to start looking for us." She slips our proof of life into the slot.

"Not comforting." I check the battery life on my phone and

pat my backpack for the portable charger. "Do we even have service in the back country?"

A spark of city girl panic over being out in the wilds of the unpaved world grows in the middle of my chest, pressing against my lungs.

"We're going on a day hike."

"To a whole other town." I pull my bag off the backseat and tug the straps over my shoulders. There's no way we could survive on the trail mix and snack bars I have packed. The two minis of Tito's vodka to celebrate our arrival at the trailhead in Crested Butte now seem like extra weight. Maybe we can use the vodka to sanitize a wound or start a fire. I probably shouldn't have dropped out of Girl Scouts after the Great Cookie Debacle of third grade when I ate over half the boxes of Thin Mints I'd sold. To other people.

Shoot. I should've packed cookies.

"You can back out now. Take the shuttle down to town in a couple of hours." Her shrug is dismissive and stings.

"No, I'm here. I'm awake. Let's do this." I pump my arms over my head like I'm at a Broncos' game. Something I've never done. Yeah, totally faking my enthusiasm.

Dressed in my beat up, gray trail runners, black leggings, and a faded Northwestern tee, I'm the picture of a reluctant outdoor enthusiast. Or college student. Mae's wearing real hiking boots, olive shorts and a tank. Adjusting my Rockies baseball cap, I pull my braids through the hole at the back.

"You packed booze in your bag, didn't you?" Her hand lifts my bag to test its weight. "Anything else?"

I twist away from her. "Protein bars and some trail mix, change of clothes, extra socks, toothbrush, deodorant, under-wear . . . you know, the basics."

"And?"

"Some Tito's for after."

"You didn't fill your hydration bag with vodka again, did you?"

"It's water," I huff. "One time at the end of season party at Highlands and no one lets you live it down."

"I'm not holding back your hair again." Mae dodges my lame attempt to kick her.

The first part of the trail is mostly flat, winding past the creek and around the lake. Because it's so early, the area is mostly deserted except for a few weirdos, I mean morning people, taking pictures in the crisp morning light.

These strangers wish us a great day as we pass them. So friendly so early. Weird.

I manage to mumble greetings and fake a happy smile as we trudge along the dirt path. This is going to be the longest day of my life.

"Channel your inner Cheryl Strayed," Mae instructs from her spot ahead of me. "From *Wild*."

"Is this a conspiracy? Mara told me to watch that the other night. I'd rather channel myself in a comfy seat at the movies with a bucket of popcorn with extra butter watching Reese Witherspoon in the movie."

"Boring. You've spent too long as a half a couple. Time to get out of your couch rut and experience new things."

"You know, I liked your suggestion of sleeping with a cowboy a lot better than this mountain goat fantasy."

"Moose!" Mae's voice rises in excitement.

"Okay, fine, your moose fantasy."

"Shh."

"I'm sure the next Ansel Adams back there doesn't really think you have actual fantasies about moose. I mean, how would that even work?" I slam into Mae's back because she's stopped in the middle of the trail.

"Shh." She fumbles and reaches behind herself, trying to cover my mouth.

Unable to breathe with her palm over both my nose and mouth, I peel away her fingers. "What is wrong with you?"

Without speaking, or removing her hand from all up in my face, she points ahead of us a few feet and to the left.

I immediately begin backing up, tugging her along with me by the straps of her pack.

When Mae said moose, I didn't think she meant an actual, living, breathing, giant rack of horns, enormous male moose standing a body length away from us.

Off the top of my head I can't quote the number of people killed by moose in an average year, not including Canadians, because I'm sure their moose to human ratio is much higher than ours, but I really don't want to become a statistic.

Or a cautionary tale.

I know I'm holding my breath and Mae is too as we slowly creep backward.

Mister Moose lifts his head from where he's eating some tasty leaves off of a shrub and stares directly at us. I can almost see his eyelashes. He blinks, and we freeze.

"Do we play dead?" I whisper close to Mae's head.

"No. Slow and steady. Keep moving away."

The sedan-sized beast lifts his snout to sniff the air. Probably deciding if we're a threat. I don't think moose are omnivores, but death by trampling isn't something I want to add to my obituary.

With a shake of his head, the moose steps away from his breakfast.

Mae grabs my arm as we turn to statues, watching for his next move, and waiting for our impending death.

Debate flashes in his bottomless black eyes right before he takes his first step.

Toward the water.

We remain frozen as he meanders away until he's up to his knees in the chilly lake.

I'm ready to turn back for the car, text everyone I know an exaggerated retelling of our encounter, drive to the nearest bar, and call it a day.

"Come on, let's get past him while we can." Mae's on the move. In the wrong direction. Up the mountain. Putting the moose between us and all modern civilization not requiring hours of walking to get to.

"I'm going to be honest with you. That sounds like a terrible idea." Unless she's planning to walk to Snowmass, and even then, the car is only a few hundred yards away. Probably less. Even I could run the distance without breaking a sweat.

"Don't let one moose ruin our fun. He's not interested in us." Why doesn't she sound terrified? She must be in shock.

"I wasn't thinking of asking him out on a date. Is it a bad omen we've already run into a creature the size of a car, who could kill us three different ways, and we're not five minutes into this adventure?" I stand in the middle of the path, staring at the moose—torn between flaking out on my friend and living to a ripe old age.

"I wouldn't hang around here if I were you," a male voice warns from behind me.

I spin and come face to chest with a tall guy. His gray T-shirt hangs off of broad shoulders and his cargo shorts end above strong calves covered in a light thatching of brown hair. The hiking boots on his feet are broken-in and caked with dried mud of varying depths. A bedroll and backpack complete his REI catalog model look.

After cataloguing his outfit, I drag my eyes up to his face. In dark sunglasses and a faded green baseball cap, only his lower face visible. A thick multiple day scruff covers his jaw and a faded cut on his bottom lip barely has a scab.

"Are you coming or going?" I ask, not sure why it matters. He's clearly one of those loner types who can live off of a few berries, a stream full of trout, and a box of quinoa for a month.

"Been in the back country for a few days, so I'm not really sure which." A deep rumble of a laugh softens his words. "Not that it matters to the moose."

Like he knows we're talking about him, the moose lifts his head and snorts.

"If you're coming down, can you tell me if you ran into more like this one up ahead?" I want to know what to expect.

"This little guy? He's a juvenile male. Nothing too much to worry about. It's the mommas with their calves you want to worry about. Elk calving season is over, so you shouldn't have any issues with them. Other than a few bears, the only critters around this trail are the beavers."

I choose to ignore the bear comment. "Great. Beavers."

"Unless one chomps down a tree and it lands on your head, you'll probably be okay." His chuckle pours out of him like slow honey. He's laughing with me, because he thinks I'm joking. Better than laughing at me. I guess.

Mae returns and stops beside me. "Who's your new friend?"

I have no idea. "He was just warning me to not loiter by the moose."

"Excellent advice. Shall we go?" Mae studies the helpful stranger.

"Have a safe hike, ladies. I'm headed home." He dips the front of his baseball cap. "Watch out for the beavers."

"Thanks for the tip." I wave as we turn away.

Once we're a few feet up the trail, Mae mumbles, "Sounds like you wanted more than just the tip."

"What? No. I wasn't even flirting with him. Unwashed and happy to sleep on the ground aren't top of my list in qualities

I look for in a man."

"He's probably not homeless, if that's what you're worried about. He was cute."

"You couldn't even see his face."

"He had nice shoulders. A man's shoulders can tell you a lot about his character."

Mae's a nut. There's no other explanation.

"Explain why you have such a theory?" I fall in step behind her as the path narrows in the trees and begins winding away from the lake.

"Does he work out? Or are his muscles from physical work? There's a difference. Are the muscles for show or strength? Avoid the 'roid users who are compensating for something. Is he a shoulder sloucher? What's he hiding? Or does he stand confidently with his shoulders back. Personally, I never trust a man with narrow shoulders."

She lists all the things shoulders reveal about a man as we hike up, up, up, passing another lake reflecting the maroon peaks dusted with white snow. When we stop for water and a snack in a flower filled meadow, she switches to men's hands.

"A man's hands tell you the story of his life. Well-groomed and baby soft? Calloused? Thick and strong? Narrow and elegant? They're the first thing I notice."

"Not his face or height? Or hair color? His hands?" I stare down at my own hands. They serve me well. To earn money to live. To create art. But I wouldn't say they're remarkable. Other than I never get a manicure and could probably give my cuticles more love. "Let me see your hands."

She lifts her hands in front of me.

"I don't think I've ever noticed before. You have long fingers and nice nail beds."

"Thanks. My point is, you need to figure out what kind of man you want. Someone who does physical work or sits in a climate controlled office all day? If you pay attention to shoulders and hands, you can rule out a lot of bad choices immediately."

"Hiker back there had nice shoulders. The cut on his lip was a little concerning. Like he's the kind of guy who gets into fights in bars. Except he said he's been hiking for three days."

"See? Pay attention to the details and they'll start to tell a story of the person behind the pretty face or fancy job title."

I lose myself in thinking about the men I know as we reach the apex of the trail. We're above the tree line surrounded by scree slides of dusty red rocks and pale green meadows. A few white columbine flowers dot the scrubby, low grass.

The landscape feels foreign and not of this planet. Above us puffy clouds float across the deep sapphire sky. I'm relieved there's no threat of rain or thunderstorms while we're exposed up here.

Both Mae and I are quiet as we traverse a rock-strewn slope. I'm still thinking about hands and shoulders to the point the kids' song is on a loop in my head: hands, shoulders, knees . . . and tips. Okay, I've modified the lyrics a little to fit our conversation.

Neil's fit, a great skier, but his hands are soft and better manicured than mine. Something about his metrosexual grooming always bugged me, but I brushed it off as me being superficial. Turns out it was more about him than me.

My mind brings up the image of a cowboy's hand gripping the horn of his saddle, or looped with a leather rein or rope. Sure, they wear gloves, but I bet their hands are slightly rough with callouses.

And I wonder how those fingers would feel on my naked skin. Would they be rough like sandpaper as they skimmed my breast or parted my thighs? Or would there be a balance between a gentle touch and the underlying strength?

"It's all downhill from here." Mae's voice interrupts my

thoughts. "We should have plenty of time to check out Crested Butte before dinner."

"I need a hot bath and some Ibuprofen." I lift and drop my shoulders, then stretch my arms in front of me, one over the other.

"Nothing a margarita and some good food can't cure." She stops at a trail sign. "Or we can head over to the hot springs."

The sign says five miles. Nope. No way. "Ten more miles? Not happening. Plus, we have zero food or shelter."

"I bet we could find some hot guys to share their tent with us."

"That sounds exactly like the start of a horror movie." I step around her. "Last one to the trailhead buys dinner."

I manage to jog a few yards before my calves start screaming at me in reminder of the miles we've already walked and the thousands of feet of altitude we've gained and lost.

When we finally reach the trailhead, the welcomed sign of a paved road up ahead greets us. I consider kissing the asphalt. I shrug off my pack and pull out my phone.

Glancing at the time, I calculate how long it's been since we started. "We've been walking for seven hours."

"Pretty good time." Mae holds up her hand for a high five.

I half-heartedly return the gesture as I find a rock to sit on while we wait for our ride to pick us up and drive us into town.

Mae bumps my shoulder. "Wake up. You're falling asleep sitting."

I blink open my eyes and stretch. "We're still out here in the middle of nowhere?"

She points at a dusty, older Jeep. "Our ride's here."

I read the lettering on the side that claims the vehicle is part of My Outdoor Adventures of a Lifetime. Ballsy claim given they don't know me. I snap a pic with my phone. Just in case.

The older guy inside waves and grins at us, but I like to err on the side of potential death versus blindly trust strangers.

After introducing himself, Chad chats us up about our hike, asking questions and giving enthusiastic responses as if we're the first people he's ever picked up who walked the trail. People like him must be born with a specific gene the rest of us don't have that allows them to live in an infinite loop of positivity.

I bet Chad's never eaten a whole pity cake with his hands before. He probably doesn't even like cake.

The colorful buildings of downtown Crested Butte greet us as we drive down the busy main street.

"What's the hustle and bustle all about? Something going on today?" Mae asks as we pass sidewalks crowded with people.

"Rodeo's in town tonight. Could be that."

Chad's not aware of the panty destroying bomb he's just dropped in my lap.

"Oh really?" Mae pinches my leg right above the knee. "What time does it start?"

He gives us the details as he stops in front of a small boutique hotel. Unfortunately, he keeps talking, sharing where to get the best green chile stew, the best gelato, the best coffee. Evidently, he's the love child of Yelp and Trip Advisor.

"Okay, well we don't want to take up any more of your time. Thanks for the ride." Mae waves a folded twenty dollar bill between the seats.

He takes the money. "You didn't have to. I'll be back tomorrow at nine to drive you home to Aspen."

"Great." I widen my mouth into a super fake grin.

Mae steps out of the backseat and I spill out after her. My legs feel like I'm a newborn giraffe. I'm stiff and gangly. She laughs as she shoves me in front of her into the hotel lobby.

"First, we rehumanize ourselves. Second, we find margaritas."

"Third, rodeo," I add.

"Your cowboy might not be at this one."

"I don't have a cowboy. I'm an equal opportunity fan."

"Uh huh. Sure." She walks toward the check-in desk in the colorful, updated Victorian lobby.

She's right. Black hat is definitely my favorite.

As soon as we're in our room, I flop face first on the closest bed, keeping my dirty boots off the pristine white duvet.

"Never mind. Cowboys or not, I'm never moving from this bed again." The soft down pillows swallow my words. "Do they have room service?"

"First dibs on the shower." Mae drops her daypack on the floor. Her weight dips the mattress when she sits. The muffled thud of her hiking shoes hitting the floor is the last thing I hear.

NINE

ZOE

DROPS OF COLD water hit the back of my legs, pulling me back to consciousness.

I shuffle deeper into the pillows and mumble, "More sleep."

"Get up, Goldilocks. We have cowboys to ogle in two hours."

My eyes flash open at the reminder of where I am. Groaning, I attempt to roll over and realize I'm still wearing my backpack. Now I'm arched over it like a turtle on his back. "Can you bring the rodeo here? I'm not sure I can walk."

"It was only eleven miles." She has the nerve to smile.

"How many steps on a Fitbit is that?" I need some context.

"Over twenty thousand."

"Slap some butter on me, I'm toast. Remind me again why we didn't drive here?" Slipping my arms through the shoulder straps, I shift off the bed. Instead of standing, I slide to the floor and drag my pack next to me.

Mae sits on her bed in a crisp white robe; warm jasmine hovers around her in a cloud of fresh, clean scent. I'm still covered in sweat and mountain grime.

I extract the contents of my bag, hoping somehow a cute outfit magically appears at the bottom. Setting aside the vodka, I toss the rest onto the floor with a sigh. Other than the oversized sloth T-shirt I plan to sleep in, I have jeans and another boring T-shirt for tomorrow along with my favorite brown strappy sandals. Fine for catching a ride home, but not for catching a cowboy. "I have nothing to wear."

Mae inspects the pile. "You're right."

"Do you think I can wear—"

"No. You smell. Pretty sure your leggings smell, too." Wrinkling her nose, she stops me from finishing. "You're lucky I overpack."

I catch the embroidered, flowy, rose tunic she tosses at me. "It's a little heavy on the boho look, but better than your sloth tee."

"You're such an adult." I offer the word as a compliment. "I'll even go down the hall for ice as a thank you."

"Shower first. Please."

Giving my upper arm a not-so-covert sniff, I agree.

I spend a long time using all the bath products and steaming up the small but elegant bathroom. Pink, shiny, and fresh, I wrap myself in a fluffy robe of my own and slip on the pair of cotton slippers. This is the life I'm cut out for.

Steam billows into the room when I open the door. "I feel human again."

Mae hands me a glass of clear, bubbly liquid accented with a lime.

"You found garnishes?" I ask, eyeing her jeans and simple white tee and wondering how many outfits she has in her small day pack. "Or did you pack them?"

"A single lime doesn't take up much room. Why else should I bother carrying a Swiss Army knife?" She points at the dresser where said blade rests next to a neatly sliced lime.

"To having you as a friend." I lift the glass and clink it with hers. "You're the best."

She takes a sip of her drink. "You've had a rough time. You deserve to have some fun, and in my experience, limes are often required for fun times."

"Don't tell me you're packing tequila and some salt, too." Excitement and awe sneak into my voice.

"Later. Get dressed and let's go before we're too tired to move."

The vodka helps. In record time, we're presentable and ready to be unleashed on other humans.

Two margaritas and a bowl of queso later, I'm feeling more like the best version of myself.

"Ready to giddy up?" Mae asks as we link arms outside the restaurant. The rodeo grounds are a short walk on the edge of town. What's a few more feet after all the miles from earlier?

Tequila is a magical elixir.

We join the flow of fellow rodeo enthusiasts as we make our way to the show. Before we can spot a single cowboy, the scent of horses and cattle wafts over us.

"I'm beginning to love this smell." I inhale deeply, filling my lungs with the slightly sweet scent.

Mae snorts. "You're unhinged."

The front rows of the grandstand are already filled with families and groups of women all dolled up and pretty. Not liking the competition, I narrow my eyes and give them side-long stares.

Mae's gentle laughter contradicts the hard press of her hand on my back as we climb the stairs. "Keep it moving. Plenty of man candy for everyone to go gaga over."

"How are you so calm in the face of the ultimate American man fantasy?" I ask, taking a seat four rows up, but right in the center of the arena.

"They're not a novelty for me. Suits are my weakness. Boots and jeans have lost their power over me."

"I don't know whether to feel sorry for you or admire your strength."

A microphone squawks to life and I lean forward in my seat. The gates open and tonight's competitors file out on their horses to take a lap around the dirt while the announcer introduces them.

One of the last horses to enter is a brown and white Paint. I hold my breath as I let my eyes scan up from the horse to the rider.

Broad shoulders.

Black Stetson.

"It's BB." I dig my fingers into Mae's arm.

"Ouch!" She uncurls my claw. "We're going to need beer."

"You can't leave me," I hiss at her.

"You'll be fine. Keep your clothes on and try not to yell anything inappropriate." She ducks down and sneaks out of our row.

Details from the first rodeo we attended a few weeks ago in Snowmass are a blur. I remember the hats, chaps, and a sudden obsession with forearms as strong hands gripped ropes or saddles. Sweet mother of pearl buttons, the strength in those arms and hands.

First up tonight is the solo roping competition. Never in my life did I think I could get turned on by watching a man on a horse try to loop a rope around the horns of a calf, then jump down and tie its legs.

Sounds kind of mean to the calf.

The speakers screech as the next rider is announced. "Put your hands together for four time All Around Champion, Buzz Garrison."

Buzz. Cowboy's name is Buzz. Seems appropriate because

he's been the object of my own personal buzz sessions with my new BOB, a breakup gift from Mae.

What lasts seconds in real time, slows down as Buzz and his horse release from their gate after the calf. My eyes focus in on the way Buzz uses his thick, strong thighs to squeeze and direct Cisco. When his feet kick in the stirrups to increase their speed, I think about how in command he is. Zero hesitation and complete focus. Then there are his arms. Honestly, I've never thought about a man's arms in such detail before.

His biceps curve and ball beneath the thin cotton of his pale blue plaid shirt as he loops and spins the rope above his head. He bites down on the length of rope he'll use to tie up the calf.

I'm sure PETA has a lot to say about cruelty in rodeos and I get it. My heart feels sorry for the little, wide-eyed calf.

But the way Buzz jumps from his horse after stopping the calf with the rope and then straddles it to bind its legs has me squeezing my thighs together.

It's all over in seconds. The calf looks a little dazed and I feel the same.

Buzz removes his hat and waves it at the crowd. The answering applause is thunderous. A slow, satisfied grin spreads across his gorgeous face when he sees his time.

Another first place finish. The grandstand—okay, mostly the women—jump to their feet and give him a standing ovation. "Desperado" by The Eagles plays on the PA system, and I wonder if it's Buzz's theme song. Like how baseball players have certain introduction songs they like to have played as they step up to bat.

And why "Desperado"? Is BB a loner who refuses to let someone love him?

He returns his hat to his head and dips the brim in acknowledgment of his fans. His body language reveals a mix of pride and embarrassment as he exits through the open gate. A few of his fellow competitors slap his back or shake his hand.

More cowboys try to beat his time, but none can come close to Buzz.

"Don't spill this when you stand up and start screaming again." Mae hands me a plastic cup of beer. "I had to charm my way up to the front of the line or I'd miss all the fun. Temper your expectations, it's Coors Light. No fancy brews at this rodeo."

"Thanks. Buzz won the roping contest." I sip the cold beer.

"Buzz?" She lifts her dark eyebrows.

"BB's name is Buzz."

"Figures. He's definitely buzz worthy."

I sigh, loudly. "Right?"

"Having rope bondage fantasies?"

Glancing around to make sure we're not corrupting small children, I lower my voice. "How'd you know? It's totally kinky and weird, but totally. I'm not saying I want to be tackled to the ground and have my wrists and ankles tied together, but there's something hot about the dominance."

Mae fans me with her hand. "Good thing the barrel racers are up next. You can cool down before the bronco bucking."

Nodding in agreement, I take another sip.

The women who race around barrels are all gorgeous. With long braids or ponytails, they're the picture of sun-kissed American beauty.

"Do you think the barrel racers and the cowboys hook up?" I lean close to Mae to whisper in her ear.

"Totally. It's probably a nonstop orgy every night after the rodeo finishes. Like in the circus."

I'm half nodding when the last part clicks in my brain. "Like the what?"

The crowd erupts in loud cheering for the super fast time

for the last racer.

Mae leans closer to me. "Freaky circus sex. Come on, you've never thought about this before? I bet the clowns are kinky. Then you have the lion tamers with their bossy ways and whips. All those bendy acrobats and trapeze artists? And of course, the sideshow freaks. You know they're into more than swallowing fire and swords."

I blink rapidly at my friend. "I don't know you at all."

She shrugs and takes a long pull of beer, speaking with her cup held near her mouth. "I'm not the one fantasizing about cowboy role play where I'm the cow."

Point made.

"Before rodeos, I never thought a man lasting eight seconds could ever be a good thing."

Overhearing me, the two women in front of us turn and lift their beers in salute. "Amen, sister."

We toast and laugh, sharing a universal truth.

"Your boyfriend's up next." I follow her finger to the activity across the dirt arena.

A group of men gather around one of the chutes. Inside, Buzz straddles the bronco. The horse kicks and the metallic clank echoes as the audience holds our collective breath. Gripping the wide braid of rope, Buzz signals he's ready. Another cowboy pulls open the gate and ducks behind it.

"That's gotta hurt," I say to Mae as we watch the horse kick and buck, trying to ditch both the rider and the strap around his middle.

"To who? The horse or the cowboy?"

"Both."

Buzz holds on with one hand around the thick rope while the other arm jerks through the air like a floppy doll. According to the announcer, the riders aren't allowed to touch that arm to the saddle or the rope while trying to stay atop the angry beast. Eight seconds doesn't seem like a long time. Unless you're trying to ride the equivalent of a swarm of hornets.

My favorite cowboy lasts nine seconds before he loosens the rope. Another horse and rider come up alongside him so he can dismount. He easily slides over to the other horse while the bronco runs ahead of them.

The crowd once again goes wild when he drops to his feet near the middle of the oval and waves. I'm on my feet, clapping and shouting with the rest of them.

Except Mae. Who remains seated and tugs me down by my back pocket.

"What?" I'm breathless.

"You were jumping up and down on my foot." She points between us.

"Sorry. I'm not sure I can handle the bull riding. Makes me nervous. What if the bull throws him off and then steps on his head?"

"He'll die," Mae says, drily.

"You're awful."

"I'm sure it happens. This is a dangerous, crazy business."

Great. Now I'm full of anxiety and dread watching the rest of the bronco riders finish.

"I need to pee." I stand and drain my cup. "Want another beer while I'm up?"

"Scaredy cat." Mae hands me her empty.

"If the lines for the hell potties are short, I'll be back in time."

She's completely right about me. Adrenaline spikes my blood and my heart rate feels like I've been running a 5K. Uphill.

Only a few people are waiting to take their turns in the port-a-potties. I jump in line and pray to the toilet gods for a relatively clean one while cursing my small bladder and all the liquids I've consumed this evening.

I think about which is worse as I hold my breath: using a popular port-a-potty, aka a claustrophobic hell closet, or riding a bull.

After drenching my hands in multiple pumps of sanitizer outside the hell portal, I join the even longer line for beer. From the arena behind me, I can hear the crowd clapping and the announcer giving the final results for the bronco riding.

Another first place finish for Buzz.

A couple of older men stand in the bar line ahead of me. Both wear crisp white western shirts and dark jeans so pressed they look like they were ironed with starch.

"That Garrison kid's having a helluva season, ain't he?" the more stout of the pair declares to his taller friend.

"Easy to win when you have all the money in the world buying you the best horses and time for training."

"I heard he just shows up. Doesn't work with the rest of the crews. Keeps to himself."

"Same, but he has a big operation behind him. Deep pockets with connections to California."

Both men frown at the word, like it's code for something bad.

"Even so," the shorter one says, "once he's out there, it's just him and whatever talent he has. You can't buy nine seconds on an angry horse."

His friend nods, but I get the feeling he's holding a grudge. "Not having to work an honest day like the rest of us probably helps."

Hmm. I'm tempted to tap one of them on the shoulder and ask him to spill all the details. Instead, I let them order and disappear into the crowd. This mini-field trip is taking forever as it is.

I finally order and toss a couple bucks in the tip jar.

"Here we go, cowgirls and cowboys. Our first bull rider tonight is leading the All Around standings this season. Give a huge Crested Butte round of applause for Colorado local boy, Buzz Garrison!" As soon as the emcee says the name, I'm racing back to the stands, beer spilling over my hands as I dodge and weave around people.

I'm barely back in view of the chute when it opens and one angry, ugly bull comes flying out with Buzz holding on by a thin rope. He's wearing the same black safety vest he wore for the bronco ride. A black helmet replaces his signature Stetson.

I'm relieved he's taken all the precautions. For good reason. The bull plants his front feet and lifts his sizable rear end to kick his hind legs, not once but twice. While turning and dipping his head down low.

Buzz bounces on the back like a flag flapping in a strong wind.

Some of those bounces have to hurt.

When the bull executes a near handstand and then quickly bucks up on his front legs, I hold my breath.

Releasing, his hold on the rope, Buzz flies in the air. For a few seconds he sails through the air, over the kicking legs of the bull who's just ejected him like a pilot from a jet.

"No," I shout and it sounds like I'm screaming in slow motion.

With a silent thud, Buzz lands in the dirt and remains still as the rodeo clown and a few others distract the bull.

Buzz should be moving. Getting up and out of the way of the angry mound of flesh and bone that seems ready to keep kicking ass and taking names.

The clown gets the bull to chase him in the opposite direction from Buzz. Another cowboy opens a gate and the clown darts in that direction, the bull close behind him.

My focus cuts back to Buzz, who's standing up with the help of another cowboy. He gives a half wave to the crowd before bracing his hands on his knees.

"Got the wind knocked out of himself," some random guy in a big straw hat says from next to me. Without realizing it, I've moved to the fence surrounding the dirt. I'm pressed against it, squeezed between men who could be competing tonight. They're huge and smell like hay, horse, and beer.

"Is he going to be okay?" My voice cracks with worry.

"Garrison? He's got a deal with the devil. Worst thing he might have are some bruised ribs. Don't worry your pretty face about him. He's not worth it." An older man to my left pats my shoulder.

"Oh, we're not. I'm not, I mean. I haven't even met the man." I stumble through my words. "We don't even know each other."

His eyes trail down from my face, pausing in the general vicinity of my boobs, before skimming over my hips and legs. "Sweetheart, didn't your momma warn you about cowboys?"

I stare at him, waiting for him to start laughing at his obvious joke. He doesn't.

"Find yourself a nice boy with a nine to five, two weeks of vacation a year, and a 401k kind of job. You'll save yourself a whole heap of heartbreak." He pats my shoulder again.

I see red. Like a bull with an unwanted passenger on his back.

"Thanks for the unsolicited advice. Stop touching me and I won't throw one of these beers in your face. Please."

It's his turn to stare at me. His dirty nails and ragged cuticles are still resting on my shoulder.

"I said please." I twist away from him and his hand drops to his side. "Now don't make me waste fifteen dollars' worth of semi-flat beer on making my point."

He holds up both his hands like I'm holding him up. "Don't shoot the messenger, sweetheart. Cowboys are nothing but trouble."

I'm about to tell him no woman likes to be called sweetheart by a strange man, when Mae coughs beside me.

"You need a back-up?" She casts a dirty look at the manhandler.

"No, I'm good. Saved your beer." I pass her the cup. "I might've spilled three dollars of beer with all the excitement."

Without a backward glance, I move away from the fence. "I'm not sure I can handle more excitement."

"What happened? You okay?"

"Other than thinking I watched a man get killed by a bull and then having some random old guy mansplain to me about the foolishness of loving cowboys, I'm good."

"I think there's a petting zoo on the other side of the arena. Maybe you need some animal therapy. Hug a sheep or pet a goat. I can hold your beer."

We weave our way through the thinning crowd as people focus on the bull riding action, the big finale before the winners are announced.

The petting area is empty of kids and toddlers. Inside the short fencing, a few sheep, a handful of rabbits, and a couple of pygmy goats meander around, sniffing the ground for over-looked treats.

"Can we pet them?" I ask, leaning over the fence, arms outstretched in the direction of a black and white goat.

"It's supposed to be ages ten and younger, but since we're getting ready to pack up for the night, you can hold a bunny, if you want." The teenager in a Shawn Mendes tee and mom jean shorts is evidently in charge.

I'd been hoping to hug a sheep, but I'm not going to argue when she scoops up a rabbit and hands it to me over the fence.

"Mind if I sit?" I tilt my head toward a stack of hay bales.

"Go for it. Just promise you won't try to steal it. I'll get hell if my count is off again tonight."

Mae and I meet eyes.

Again? she mouths.

With my therapy rabbit cradled in my arms, I sit on the top hay bale. Petting the softest fur ever, I start to feel better. Less ragey and full of adrenaline over a man I don't know who's crazy enough to ride bulls for a living.

"Helping?" Mae asks, sitting next to me.

"Much."

She pets my rabbit's ears.

"Um, you're going to need to get your own bunny. This one's mine." I bat her hand away.

"Greedy girl."

"Don't listen to her," I whisper to the rabbit. "I'm very nice."

"Lucky bunny." The voice over Mae's shoulder is a familiar masculine drawl.

I peek at the worn brown suede chaps and denim covered legs standing directly in front of me. My mouth goes dry as I quickly sweep my gaze past the buckle and over the blue shirt. No more vest. Finally, I'm greeted with the lazy, sexy smile of Mr. Buzz Garrison, rodeo champion and death wish haver.

"I'm sure if you ask nicely, you can pet any bunny you want." I replay that in my head and it sounds like "pet any-body." Yep, dirty.

"What if I want your bunny?" His lips spread into a wolfish grin that my traitor body thinks is hot. I don't know which is worse—his sexy full mouth or the way mischief sparkles in his dark eyes.

He did not just say that.

He did.

And the way his lips hitch up on one side, making his smile a little lopsided, tells me he meant it to sound too sexy for church talk.

Good thing it isn't Sunday.

I glance around for Mae to confirm he's standing here talking to me, but she's wandered to the far side of the petting pen.

Sneaky girl giving us privacy.

"Shouldn't you be nursing your injuries?" I manage to sound casual.

"I'm fine." He strokes the fur on the luckiest bunny ever. "Nothing that hasn't happened before."

"You looked dead."

"I'm sorry that upset you. I'm guessing you haven't been to a lot of rodeos before."

"This isn't my first one." I straighten my back.

"I know." His voice lowers to a rumble meant only for me. I stare up at him and notice a faded cut on his bottom lip.

TEN

JUSTIN

WHEN YOU CLIMB on top of a bull named Bad Blood, you're pretty much confirming you have some major issues.

I tell myself this as I reassure the crew I'm good. I adjust my riding hand under the rope, wrapping my fingers over the thick braid, my only tether to stay on this ton of rage. Giving the signal to open the gate, I dig in my heels and say a little prayer I walk away from this ride.

Breathe, I tell myself.

Riding a Great White shark might be easier than staying on Bad Blood. I try to count the seconds in my head while shifting to keep myself from going over the horns. Third rib from the bottom on my left side will always have a ridge on it from where I got stepped on by a bull smaller than this dude.

He kicks and bucks, dipping forward and tilting back. I sling my left arm over my head, using it to keep myself straddling his back. When he does a double-kick with his back legs, my weight shifts to the side and my hand slips.

Shit.

Hitting the ground shoves all the air from my lungs. Darkness closes in from the edges of my vision, as I tense for the impact of hooves on my body. This is going to hurt.

Sounds of stomping feet and yelling move farther away as I focus on trying to breathe enough air to keep from passing out. If I'm not in direct impact range, being still is the best plan. Let the clown and other cowboys distract the bull from me until they can get him through the chute.

Opening my eyes, I see Hobo Jim, tonight's clown, distracting the bull long enough for the crew to get the gate open and shoo him through it.

Thank fuck.

"Let's get you up," Gentry says, extending his hand for me to grip.

"How many second was that?" I ask as I stand with his help.

His thick gray mustache twitches when he chuckles. "Anything broken?"

"Back might be sore tomorrow considering I used it to break my fall, but I'm okay."

"Ten seconds." He answers my first question. My mentor, my trainer, and most importantly, my friend, grips my hand in his.

"Not bad. That SOB had some fancy footwork." I give a half-hearted wave to the crowd to let them know I'm okay. Hoots and hollering echo amongst the applause, along with a few embarrassing "I love you" declarations.

"Saw that. Can't have you getting too comfortable just because you have all those championship silver buckles."

"But they're so pretty," I joke with him as we leave the ring.

"Even if you think you're okay, you better walk around so you don't stiffen up. You'll need to take your victory lap pretty soon."

I'm humbled by his confidence in me. Extending my hand to shake his, I say, "I learned how to be a cowboy from you, Gent. Don't know what I'd do without you."

Tightening his hold, he nods. "The pleasure's been mine."

In spite of the twenty year age difference, he's one of my best friends. So I take his advice. Stripping off my gloves, I undo my helmet and vest. The pull in my back muscles warns me the next couple of days are going to suck. I stretch out my arms and roll my neck, making sure nothing's fucked up. Ribs seem okay as I take a deep inhale.

If Gentry thinks it'll be good enough to win tonight, I'm not going to doubt him.

Taking my time, I stroll away from the paddocks and grandstand to the far side of the ring. A few people recognize and greet me. I brush them off with a smile and keep moving.

In a quiet corner, I spot a couple of women hanging around the otherwise empty petting pen.

The pretty brunette sitting on top of a couple hay bales looks vaguely familiar. I'm guessing she's hung around a few rodeos this summer. The image of a buckle bunny holding a real life rabbit amuses me. She could be on a poster with her soft pink shirt and jeans. The braid is the cherry on top.

Rock stars have groupies, cowboys have buckle bunnies. Like magpies, they're captivated by the bright and shiny buckles. Some of them steal the buckles and wear them around. I guess it's like wearing a player's jersey.

Some of the guys have no respect for the bunnies. Sure, they'll flirt with them and fuck them, but the shit they say when it's just us guys around makes my skin crawl. I don't participate or condone it. Hell, I've had guys throw punches at me for standing up for a woman and her reputation.

We're all consenting adults around here. Even the young bucks, the guys barely eighteen and on the circuit for the first time. Away from home, being offered sex seemingly without strings can mess with a guy's head. Both of them if he's stupid enough not to wear a condom.

Guys like Gentry have seen it all. Every dumbass, idiot bullshit a guy can pull. They don't stand for stupidity. I know because I was a dumb buck when I first started competing, too.

So that's why I hesitate to start a conversation with the familiar brunette holding a rabbit. I avoid the bunnies, no matter if my reputation says otherwise. I make the decision to keep walking, but my body and mouth don't get the signal.

"Lucky bunny," I say under my breath.

Beautiful deep brown eyes from my fantasies flash to mine. She says something about asking nicely to pet her bunny. I think that's what she says. I'm too caught up in her eyes and her full, rosy lips.

"What if I want your bunny?" I want to slap myself. Loss of filter is one of the signs of a head injury. And evidently, I've lost mine. Great. I probably have a concussion.

She asks about my injuries and I brush off her concern.

I know I know her, but she's not one of the regulars. Running through the towns I've been through in the past month, I try to place here.

Jackson Hole. Cody. Cheyenne. Loveland. Steamboat. Rifle. Snowmass.

"This isn't my first rodeo," she says, annoyed.

Snowmass.

"I know."

A couple of weeks ago, she and a group of friends stopped by after the show, hung around waiting to be noticed. I let her feed Cisco an apple. I remember her because she acted nervous around horses.

Slowly her eyes trail up my legs and torso to my face.

I hold her gaze. "You fed my horse an apple a couple of weeks ago in Snowmass."

And I saw you yesterday on the trail, but I keep this information to myself. If she doesn't recognize me, I'm happy to keep my private life separate from the rodeo world.

At least until I get to know her better.

"You remember?" Her voice sounds slightly breathless.

Guess even outside the circuit, cowboys have reputations for short attention spans and bad memories.

"Cisco hasn't shut up about it. Keeps asking when we're going to see you again." I give her a genuine smile.

She plays along, "Really? I didn't realize I made such an impression on your horse."

I stroke the bunny, which means my fingers are inches from touching her hands, her lap, and just south from the bottom curve of her breasts. I'm crossing a line into her personal space, but she hasn't shifted away.

"If I don't bring you over to say hi, I'm not sure he'll ever forgive me. The last thing I need is a moody horse, pining after a beautiful woman."

She huffs out a disbelieving laugh. "Wow, does that line work for you?"

"You tell me." I've come this far with the cheesy lines, why turn back now? If I am concussed, I probably won't remember this conversation tomorrow. Which is a good thing, because I think I'm about to eat dirt on this flirtation.

Tilting her head to the side, she studies me. With the bunny in her arms, and her fingers slowly stroking through the fur, she could be a villainess. She's definitely dangerous.

I feel her appraisal of me and know I'm about to come up short. This woman might dress country, but there's something different about her. I doubt she's after a shiny buckle and bragging rights. There's a story in her eyes, a sadness hidden behind her smile.

Curiosity tugs at my chest, pushing me to continue talking

with her. It's an unfamiliar feeling to want to know more about a woman at a rodeo.

Might be because I'm a shallow, cocky bastard. Or because I've kept my walls up so long, they're covered in ivy and thorny brambles.

Not trusting people is in my blood. My family keeps to ourselves to protect our secrets. I have a hard time letting people in, but there's something about her smile that makes me want to open the door.

"Guess I need to go break Cisco's heart. Y'all enjoy the rest of your evening," I drawl, purposely pouring on the charm as I reach up to tip my hat.

Only I'm not wearing a hat.

I try to pass it off like I'm going to run my fingers through my hair, but with my buzz cut I don't have much of that either. I'm left with sweeping my palm down my head. Feeling completely off my game, I glance down at her perched on the hay bale.

Blinking her dark lashes, she snuggles the bunny's head. "You don't play fair."

Waiting to see what she does next, I stuff my hands in my front pockets and rock back on the thick heels of my boots.

"Let's go see Cisco." She scoops up the fluff ball and then stands before setting it on the ground in the pen. "Mae, this man wants to show me his horse. I'm almost positive it's not a euphemism, but if I'm not back in ten," she glances at me, "five minutes, you'll know where to find me."

I grin in spite of the vague insult of my character. Gentry's eardrum-splitting whistle pierces the din from the crowd and speakers. "Better make it ten. I have a belt buckle to collect."

Holding out my elbow, I gesture for her to take my arm. "It'll make Cisco's day if he knows you're watching him from the stands."

"Right. The horse will know I'm there." Her laugh is dry, questioning my sanity no doubt, but she loops her arm through mine.

"Horses are like elephants. They never forget a pretty face." I lead us back toward the stalls and stop next to where Cisco is saddled and ready for me. "Or a name."

I let the words hang between us, hoping she'll offer her name and not make me ask.

"Zoe."

"Nice to meet you, Zoe." My smile is slow and genuine. "I'm Justin."

Her eyebrows draw together.

"Everyone calls me Buzz because of this." I brush a hand over my head.

"Nice to meet you, Justin."

My name is called as tonight's champion. I reluctantly release her arm. Stepping into the stirrup, I swing my leg over Cisco's back and settle into my saddle. "Meet me at the Main Street Bar. I'll be there as soon as I finish up around here."

As the group of riders line up in the center of the arena, I catch a glimpse of Zoe's dark braids in the crowd. I fight the smile tugging on my lips. Seeing her again makes me happy—unexpected, but not unwelcome.

As I take my slow lap to show off the winner's buckle, I catch myself tracking her. Tonight's emcee thanks everyone for coming and the music cuts to some country song I don't bother to recognize.

Kimmy and Cheryl, two of the barrel riders on the circuit, stroll my way as I remove Cisco's saddle and tack. Both women are nice enough, on the eyes and personality, but neither is the woman I'm hoping to spend the rest of the evening with. Same with the rest of the crew and riders. Not a bad bunch of people, but honest to God, I can't spend another night listening to the same stories and exaggerated triumphs.

I'm quick to finish up with Cisco and put him in the paddock where he'll stay overnight with some of the other horses.

"Coming to the bar tonight?" Kimmy, the freckled blonde, asks. Cheryl, a taller blonde with long legs and a longer list of conquests, leans against the fence near me.

"You haven't hung out with us all summer." Cheryl pouts.

"Been busy." I close and lock the horse trailer. "Beautiful women like you two have your pick of cowboys on the circuit. No reason to waste your time on a boring old guy like me."

The two women exchange glances.

"If you change your mind, we're going to Main Street," Kimmy says with a wave as they walk away.

Well, shit. I've invited Zoe to meet me at the same place. The longer I take to finish for the night, the longer she and her friend will be in a bar full of adrenaline high cowboys.

Gentry doesn't complain or ask questions when I borrow his RV's bathroom to clean up.

After the world's quickest shower and a change of clothes, I catch a ride downtown with Dusty, who can't wipe the surprise off his face.

"Someone smells fresh." He nods in approval. "You hooking up with the buckle bunny you chatted up earlier? Is that the same one from Snowmass?"

I arch an eyebrow. "You making a scrapbook of my life?"

He fakes a laugh. "Thought you swore off the bunnies."

"She's not a buckle collector." Now he's starting to ruin my good mood.

"If you say so." He pulls into a spot in the parking lot. "Nothing wrong with a woman who knows what she wants."

He makes a good point.

"Thanks for the ride. Remember to wear one of these to-night." I pick up the open box of condoms from the floor. "Might want to go ahead and put one on now."

He flips me off as I toss the box on the seat.

Still chuckling, I open the door and hop out of the truck's cab.

"Thanks, Dad," he yells while I walk away.

Inside the dimly lit bar, I weave my way through the crowd, scanning for Zoe. A half wall divides the dining area from the long bar. Beyond the bar is a dance floor at the back.

After making a loop around the space, I finally spot two cowboys already chatting up Zoe and her friend near the front of the bar.

As I watch, the men act like roosters with their puffed up chests. If they weren't chatting up the woman I'm interested in, I'd probably find their cocky preening funny.

Frowning, I stroll up to the foursome.

"Hello, ladies." I flash a bright smile at Zoe.

Her eyes light up as she scans over my body.

"Someone cleans up well." Her friend extends a hand. "I'm Mae."

"Justin," I introduce myself. "Nice to meet you."

Releasing Mae, I turn to Zoe and take her hand, lifting it to my lips.

Her eyes widen when I press a kiss to her skin.

"Thanks for coming out tonight," I drawl, soft enough only she can hear me.

Her lips part and she blinks slowly at me. I smile at the effect I have on her.

Good, because she's all I can think of right now.

"Save a dance for me," the bolder of the two men tells Zoe.

"I'll be happy to show you how to two-step."

"I think I have it covered." I cast a dirty look over my shoulder.

When the two young bucks blanch at my scowl, I struggle to keep from laughing. Best part about having a reputation as a cranky bastard, people don't want to get on my bad side.

Positioning my body between the guys and Zoe, I ask, "Hungry? Let's find a seat."

We grab a table in the corner. Out of habit I sit with my back against the wall to watch the room and avoid anyone sneaking up on me.

A four piece band takes the tiny stage and introduces themselves. The group of older men with silver in their beards warms up and does a quick sound check. The music is loud enough to prevent conversation. A few couples dance to the classic country songs.

Not that I could talk much as I inhale a bison burger like it's my first meal in a month. Zoe and Mae pick at a bowl of chips and guacamole while drinking margaritas. I'm the beast among beauties.

One of the guys from earlier stalks over to our table. He's either stupid or lost a bet.

"I'm here to see if you're ready to dance." Luckily for him, he directs his question at Mae.

She smiles at him and then gives Zoe a questioning glance.

"Go ahead." Zoe encourages her with a smile. "You get your two-step on."

I stare at her while the cowboy leads her friend to the dance floor. "Not a fan of country music?"

"Not really. And I don't know the dances."

A few couples clearly have the steps down as they glide around the dance floor.

Several cowboys in the bar keep glancing over here. I'm not

sure if they're shocked to see me with a woman or if they're checking out Zoe. Neither option sits well with me. To squash their interest in her, I'm going to need to make a statement. And that's going to push me out of my comfort zone.

"That shouldn't stop you." Resolved, I wipe my hands on my napkin and stand. "Come on, I'll show you."

"You're asking me to dance?" She stares at my outstretched fingers.

I wiggle them. "I've been told I'm good, so I can promise I won't step on your toes."

She studies my face, her eyes searching for something. Sincerity? Joking?

"I'm serious. Don't women like men who can dance? Or is that something my grandmother told me to get me to take lessons?" Cocking my head, I give her a half smile.

"Now I'm curious." She slips her hand into mine, and I pull her up.

Holding her hand, I guide us through the tables to the edge of the dance floor. I haven't danced in a long time. Can't remember the last time. Maybe my grandmother's seventy-fifth birthday party last year.

Let's hope I can remember the steps and not make a fool of myself.

ELEVEN

ZOE

JUSTIN'S WARM, ROUGH fingers cradle my hand like it's something precious. I blindly follow him through the bar to the dance floor. He could probably lead me right out the door and into the night, and I wouldn't protest.

It's the first time we've touched skin to skin for more than a minute, and my body responds like he's flipped a switch, flooding light where darkness has loitered for months.

The warmth from his hand around mine is the sun breaking through storm clouds.

On the small stage—only two feet higher than the rest of the floor—is a quartet of older men playing old fashioned country tunes. One has a slide guitar splayed in front of him. The tunes are upbeat, but the lyrics I catch could drive anyone to drink whiskey for breakfast.

Justin leads me to the far edge, where it's less crowded with couples rotating counter-clockwise around the floor.

"Trust me." With a jerk to my hand, he spins me around to face him. He lifts my left hand to his shoulder and rests his on my back near my bra strap. It's a formal position with lots of room between our bodies for the Holy Spirit. Or at least the big gap makes me think of dancing supervised by Catholic nuns.

"What's so funny?" The corners of his mouth curl up.

"Nothing," I say with a shake of my head. "I'm nervous."

"Don't be. I've got you." The smile he gives me is nothing but sweet and genuine.

"All I ask is you catch me before my face plants on the floor."

He barks out a chuckle. "Promise."

"Swear on your belt buckle. Or Cisco."

He's still chuckling when he meets my eyes. "Take me at my word."

Beneath his black Stetson, his eyes are dark as a night without stars. It would be so easy to get lost in them forever. He begins talking again and I try to focus on his words and not the trifecta of his eyes, his hand on my back, and mine touching his shoulder.

"We're going to go quick quick, then slow slow. Step on your right foot first." He lifts and lowers his feet to demonstrate. "Follow me. When I want you to turn, I'll put a little pressure on right here. Can you feel that?"

Yes, yes I can. I nod as he flexes his hand against my bra strap.

"Good, now open your hand and rest your palm on my shoulder."

I'm fondling his shoulder. It is everything and more. Strong, rounded with muscle, and hard as a rock. A girl could have fantasies about his shoulders. I add it to my collection.

"Here we go." He smirks.

Dancing with Justin is like skiing in fresh powder. Effortless and smooth. Even though I'm dancing backward, he leads me around the floor, weaving us through the other couples. With a gentle press of his fingers on my shoulder blade, he guides me through a turn. Amazingly, I don't trip.

"You look surprised," he whispers when I'm back in his arms.

It's an understatement for how I'm feeling right now.

I'm a minute from turning into a pile of swoony goo. Never in my life have I swooned over a man before.

But Justin isn't a regular guy.

He's a cowboy.

Who can dance and make me laugh. He could probably incinerate my clothes by reading the bar menu in that low, smooth drawl of his.

In an act of self-preservation, I find myself staring at his mouth instead of his eyes.

His tongue pokes out and presses against a barely visible cut on his lip.

My fingers flex on the wide shoulder as I stare at the almost healed cut.

Oh shit.

When the song ends, my mind is a mess of trying to fit together the hiker with the cowboy persona at the same time preventing my body from stripping off all my clothes right here and now. I'm turned on and freaking out.

"How'd you like it?" he asks, as we walk toward the bar.

Quick, quick. Slow.

I'll take it both ways.

"You're an amazing dancer."

"And you're a quick learner." I catch his smile from the corner of my eye.

Quick, quick. Slow.

I focus on finding Mae in the crowd of cowboy hats. When I finally pick her out, I make a beeline in that direction.

"Can I get you something from the bar?" Justin offers.

Why does he have to be nice as well as sex in a cowboy hat?

"I think I've hit the wall. I'm going to grab Mae and head back to the hotel." Sure, I'm using my friend as a human shield, but she'd do the same if the roles were reversed. "Thanks for the dance."

Mae's laughing and chatting with the two guys from earlier. I swear I hear a growl come out of Justin.

"Probably a good idea. Nothing but trouble about to happen with this bunch."

My eyes widen at his words and warning tone.

Mae's less enthused about leaving.

Justin makes a comment about "charges being dropped" and remarkably, both guys suddenly have somewhere else to be.

"We should go," I say to Mae, silently telling her with my eyes not to argue.

Reluctantly, she finally agrees. I apologize to Justin.

"No problem. I hope our paths cross again." He leans close to give me a kiss on the cheek. The brim of his hat bumps my head.

If Mae doesn't speed up, I'm thinking about dragging her out of here. Or flipping her over my shoulder and carrying her out like a sack of potatoes.

"Hurry up." My voice is whiny and pleading. Yet she still doesn't pick up on the fact I need to go. Now. Or sooner if possible.

"What's wrong with you?" She digs in her heels, making it almost impossible for me to keep on my trajectory toward the exit.

Stubborn, stubborn woman. I yank on her arm.

"Why are you running away from the cute cowboy who was all over you? Isn't that the end game here?" Her voice is teasing as she wiggles free, and stops near the front door.

"I'll tell you when we get back to the hotel."

The way she stares at me, either the top of my head is on

fire, or she's checking to see if I've lost my mind. "No. Nope. Uh huh. Spill."

It doesn't even make sense to me. I've been having sexy dreams about cowboys, ropes, and me for weeks. Now here I am, with a live one on the end of my line. Wait, that's a fishing metaphor. I've got one in my lasso? Sure. Point is, he's not just a cowboy.

"Remember the friendly hiker?"

"Moose patrol?" She crosses her arms. "Don't tell me you've already moved on from cowboys to wilderness men. Outdoor enthusiasts? Backcountry Romeo stole your heart with his unhygienic charms?"

"It's the same guy. Or I'm so tired, I'm hallucinating."

"Are you sure? Buzz is clean shaven."

"Men shave. Sometimes they even shower. It can happen. I recognized the cut on his lip."

Mae squints and dips her chin. "The cut. On his lip."

"I think." Cowboys and their dates congregate outside on the sidewalk, stalling our getaway. "Once I thought they were the same guy, I got awkward. He probably thinks I'm a weirdo."

"I don't get it. Now you have two things in common. Hiking and rodeos." She counts on her fingers. "And showering. Three things."

She allows me to pull her down the aisle. "You're missing the point."

I keep moving until we're across the street and the din of country music is muffled.

"Spill."

I face Mae's crossed arms and "you're crazy" judging eyes.

"Hiker said he was headed home." I wait for the pieces to click into place for her.

"So?"

"It means BB is local."

"Not to sound like an echo, but, so?" Planting her feet, she glances over her shoulder at the bar.

"My fantasy hook up can't be someone I could run into at the grocery store at ten o'clock at night in my pajamas when I'm making a run for cake, popcorn, and tampons."

"Specific list."

"It's happened before. My point is, if I'm going to have a one-night stand and live out some sort of wild sex dream, I can't see him again."

"You're not making sense. What if it's the best sex of your life? Wouldn't you want a repeat? Easier if he's local."

Somehow I know she's right. He'd be amazing and I'd totally want more than one night.

"And that's the problem. Sage is right. I'm not cut out for random hookups. He's a hot rodeo cowboy. I'm not a buckle bunny. He probably beds a different woman in every town he visits." My heart misses a beat as disappointment fills my chest. "I'm not ready to be a notch in a belt. I'm a mess. I spent five years loving the wrong man for me."

"I still think being properly sexed up by the right man for one night is the cure you need."

"Can't I be smudged with a sage bush instead? I'll even let someone sweep feathers all over my body while screaming chakra realignment chants."

Mae links her arm through mine. I freeze for a second thinking she's going to drag me back to Buzz. Thankfully, she spins us in the direction of our hotel.

"You know that's not a thing. The screaming part. Your best friend is a green smoothie, soft hearted, blessings kind of woman."

"She'd happily burn sage around my body, probably blowing smoke in my face and everything." I miss my bestie. I've yet to figure out the time difference to the other side of the world so we can FaceTime instead of sending random videos and voice messages.

"Then it's good you have me."

"I don't know what I'd do without you." It's true. I'd be stuck hiding out in a hotel in Crested Butte waiting for driver guy Chad to come get me.

Or at home, alone, and eating cake.

TWELVE

ZOE

"CHAD'S MIA." I drop my backpack at my feet and lean against the planter full of colorful flowers in front of our hotel. "He was supposed to be here forty minutes ago. We'd be halfway home by now."

After crashing upon arrival back in our room, we both slept like stones. The blasting *beep-beep-beep* of Mae's backup alarm jolted us both awake with ten minutes to spare before our pick up time.

The adrenaline of rushing to get ready has faded and now I have the yawns as we wait.

"Did I brush my teeth?" Mae leans close enough for me to smell her thankfully minty breath.

"Yes."

"I'm pretty sure my bra is on inside out." She pulls her shirt away from her chest and peers down it. "Try calling Chad again. I'm going to go fix this and find some coffee. Want some?"

"Iced with two percent if you're asking."

After she's gone, I realize I don't have Chad's number in my phone. She's been the main contact. This is when my city girl paranoia pays off. I dig up the picture of his car and expand it to read the name.

"My outdoor adventures, my ass," I mumble as I enter his number. Not surprisingly, it goes straight to voicemail. There's no point in leaving a third voicemail since he hasn't responded to the first two Mae left him. "Well, Chad, you would appear to be off on your own personal adventure this morning."

I do the mature thing and stick my tongue out at my phone before setting it on the planter next to my hip. Nothing to do but wait for Mae to return with coffee. Once she's back, we can figure out our options. Top options right now are: hitchhiking, calling someone at home and asking them to give up three hours of their life, or finding another Chad.

I put on my sunglasses and then pick a stray white thread off my dark jeans. A lock of hair falls over my forehead when I dip my head. I push it back into the nest of a bun. The braid from last night still exists in theory. The ends are wrapped into a ball near the nape of my neck.

Even behind my sunnies, I need to squint. The strong summer sun at this elevation is way too bright for nine thirty in the morning. Despite showering, I look like I finished walking a half marathon five minutes ago. If we're out here for much longer, I'm going to need to find some shade.

Remembering my cap, I unbuckle it from the side of my pack and tug it on my head. Not my best look, but I'm not here to impress anyone.

I try Chad's number again. Voicemail.

"You suck," I tell my phone's screen.

"Need a ride?" a guy in a truck yells in my general direction.

Glancing up, I'm already waving him away. "No, just waiting for a friend."

My wave stalls mid-air in a sad, solo jazz hand.

A huge gray truck with those double rear wheels is stopped in front of the hotel. Behind the truck sits a horse trailer. There's no way they're not blocking traffic as the driver leans closer to the passenger window.

"Sure you're okay?" The voice is as familiar as the buzzed head and full lips. Deep brown eyes peer down at me from above the same Ray-Bans he wore hiking yesterday.

A car honks and Justin gestures for them to pass him.

"We meet again, Cowboy," Mae purrs as she hands me a large iced coffee.

Inside the cab, he gives her a small salute.

Mae coughs to cover the muttered "go with it" she says for only my ears. "So glad I ran into you while getting coffee. Seems our ride's still MIA. You might be the right man for the job."

More car horns honk down the street while I silently curse her.

Justin waves his arm out the window to tell people to pass him. "If you're joining me, we should probably go before the good people of Crested Butte riot."

"You're our hero." Mae has both our packs in her hand, and steps off the curb before I can process she's accepted his offer.

"We don't want to trouble you. We're probably not even going in the same direction you're headed." Making excuses, I remain standing by the planter. "I'm sure our ride will be here soon."

Mae opens the door, tosses both bags on the back seat, and climbs in the back. "Stop the nonsense and come on."

I glance at my phone again, for some stupid reason hoping Chad responded. Yes, I'm thinking Chad is a better option than being squished up against the cowboy who's starring in my recent fantasies. Give me enough time and I'll come up with a reason why.

"You know I'll leave you here." She widens her eyes and rolls them toward Justin, who sits in the driver's seat wearing an amused half-smile.

"I promise I'm not a kidnapper." He pats the seat next to him.

It's a big truck with a roomy king cab, but once we climb in and I shut the door behind us, it feels tiny.

I bobble my iced coffee and almost dump the entire thing over the center console into Justin's lap.

"Whoa there, watch it." He stabilizes my cup with his hand over my fingers. Memories of him holding me while we danced last night flood my body with zings.

"You got it?" He's still holding my cup upright.

"Huh?"

"Zoe's usually able to hold her beverages all by herself." Mae teases from the backseat, breaking the intimate bubble around Justin and me.

"I got it."

"Good." He checks his mirrors and pulls into traffic. "So where are we going?"

"Home," I say.

"Figured as much. Can you give me a little more information? I didn't bring my ruby slippers." Amusement softens his words.

Mae's head appears between the seats. "We left my car at Maroon Bells when we hiked over yesterday, but you probably already knew that. You can drop us at Zoe's condo in Aspen."

I turn my head to stare at her.

She nods and grins.

"Thought I recognized you from the trail." Justin meets my gaze and I know he remembers our encounter. "Condo in Aspen. That's pretty fancy."

"I have a roommate." The lie bubbles out of me. From the corner of my eye I can see Mae shift in the backseat to stare at me.

"Makes sense." He nods, accepting my word. Because why

wouldn't he? "Where are you from?"

"Chicago," I answer. Small talk I can handle. "You?"

"Colorado, mostly."

"I'm the weirdo. Born and raised around Aspen. True local. Although I moved back last winter for the ski season, I'm still here," Mae adds.

Justin twists to address Mae. "I thought you looked familiar."

"I waitress around town. You've probably seen me in one of the local restaurants."

He shakes his head. "Aspen's too fancy for my blood. Unless you work at Hickory House, I doubt it."

"I love it there. Their pulled pork gives me life." I'm practically drooling.

"I'm a rib man, myself, but it's nice to see a good place stick around." Even without looking directly at him, I can see Justin's grin.

"Isn't it a cliché for a cowboy to hang out at the local barbecue joint?" Mae asks, and I want to elbow her.

"Some clichés are true. If I could tie up Cisco, I'd probably ride into town. I bet there's a city council ordinance now about no horse parking. Shame for an old silver town to forget men on horses put it on the map."

"You must live close to town if you could ride in for dinner." I'm not fishing to find out where he lives. Just curious.

"Normally I keep that information private, especially with people I meet at rodeos, but since we're all neighbors, I'll tell you."

"You don't have to. I mean, we'd never show up at your house or anything. We're not weirdos." My words argue against the point I'm trying to make.

His laughter is rich and deep when it fills the cab. "Thanks for clarifying."

"Sweet lord," Mae mumbles under her breath.

I don't know if he hears her, but his laughter softens. "I live up at the Easy Z ranch. At least when I'm not on the road during the summer."

"What a coincidence!" Over-enthusiastically, Mae pats my shoulder. "That's Zoe's rapper name."

"More like a college nickname," I mumble, a lame attempt at a joke.

Silence fills the cramped space.

"Which one of you is joking?" he asks with a straight face.

THIRTEEN

JUSTIN

I CAN'T TELL if Zoe's joking about being called Easy Z.

If she had a wild past, I'm not judging. If you haven't had a wild period in your life, you're probably not living to the fullest.

"More likely to be my rapper name." Her smile doesn't reach her eyes. "I didn't go crazy in college. Unless you call spending all nighters watching a kiln wild."

"You're an artist?"

"Massage therapist." She wiggles her fingers in front of her. "The only magic I create these days involves these puppies and some body oil."

I jerk the wheel and the tires vibrate over the rumble strip on the shoulder as I imagine her wrapping her fingers around me.

"That sounded really dirty." Zoe laughs, sounding embarrassed. "I don't give those kind of massages. I swear."

"This is the second time recently you've had to clarify that. I'm a little concerned." Mae's voice holds genuine worry.

"Definitely frowned upon at the spa at the Ritz. Like joy and laughter." Zoe forms an x with her arms. "Relaxation must be serious."

If she means the Ritz Carlton, she works at a high-end

place. Even if she makes bank with tips, there's no way she could afford a condo to herself in Aspen. From the corner of my eye I study her. She definitely doesn't come across as hoity, but there must be money there. Either she has family money or a rich boyfriend. Maybe even a sugar daddy.

The last two options sour my stomach. We've barely spoken, and she ghosted last night, but I'm intrigued. Hell, after dancing with her, I might even be smitten.

I haven't felt a spark in a long time.

When women throw themselves at the rodeo, there's no chase. No desire to get to know each other before tumbling into bed, or the nearest wall. I miss the slow burn of getting to know a woman, discovering ways to make her smile and finding out what makes her laugh. Uncovering how to make her eyes light up. And after all of that, putting that knowledge to use bringing her pleasure. Satisfied in knowing I can make her happy.

When I was younger, I only focused on what I wanted. Summers spent as a good looking young buck on the circuit twisted my perception about relationships. Easy sex at a young age definitely warped my view on love. Coming home to the ranch permanently, with the responsibility of preserving it, has changed me. Life's too short to live only for yourself.

"Why the rodeo?" Zoe asks.

"Besides the promise of a new belt buckle?" I tilt my head toward the driver's window and glance at her.

"Seems like risking your life is a lot for bragging rights."

"I like the challenge. I don't compete against the other riders. My focus is on beating my high score."

"Have you ever been hurt?" Mae asks.

"All the time. My back's still a little sore from last night."

"You should have Zoe give you a massage." Mae suggests. "I'm sure she'll give you the friends and family discount."

Zoe casts a dirty look over her shoulder at her friend.

"Or not," Mae says.

"I have a physical therapist down valley. He's a sadist who uses torture devices on me."

Zoe's shoulders drop, evidently relieved I'm not taking Mae serious. I'm not sure how to interpret her reaction. We settle into a semi-comfortable silence as I carefully navigate the twists in the road.

"Feel free to play DJ," I suggest to Zoe. "I think most of the presets are country, but there's satellite on there, too."

"Who says I don't like country?" She gives me a flirty smile.

I flash a grin. "The fact that you have a rapper name?"

"Mae likes to tease me about being from the big city. I think she confuses gangster with gangsta."

"So, you're an Italian mafia princess?" I ask, not even half serious.

Mae snorts from the backseat.

Zoe shakes her head. "Don't even joke about it. I have an uncle who we all swear is in the mob. Or based his entire life on *The Sopranos*. We're not even Italian, but you'd never know it if you met him. He even says things like 'forgeddaboutit' with a Jersey accent. The Saragossa side of my family is from Spain, but he's from Wisconsin like my mom."

"Family's weird." An uncle with a fake accent would be welcome in the Garrison family. We don't even know what normal means.

"You should meet my younger brother. Do you have siblings?" Zoe asks.

"Two younger sisters who live in California. Might see them a couple times during ski season. We're not really close. In fact, I'm only close with my grandmother."

"That's sweet," Zoe says.

"Not sure anyone would call Felecia sweet. She still heads

the family like the Queen runs England. The matriarch of the Easy Z may be in her seventies and tiny, but only a fool would knowingly cross her."

"You sound a little bit afraid of her." Mae's voice is teasing.

"Damn right I am." I chuckle. "Took me a few tries to learn that lesson, but it's one I won't forget."

Zoe lifts her eyebrows in question, but now's not the time for the Garrison family history lesson. When I don't give more information, she flips through the stations until she finds a song she likes. Figures it's Sam Hunt. Do all women have crushes on him?

"How do you feel about tacos?" I ask as we hit the outskirts of Carbondale. "I didn't have breakfast this morning and there's a great food truck in town. Nothing fancy."

Not sure I need to add the caveat. It's a food truck.

Zoe flicks her gaze to me. "Taco's sound amazing. All we've had is coffee."

"So much coffee. I really need to pee," Mae says without embarrassment.

"Not sure the taco truck has anything more than a port-a-potty."

Zoe frowns. "No more peeing outside. Please. Look, there's a McDonald's."

I'm confused. "No tacos?"

"Tacos after. McD's has excellent upkeep on their bathrooms. Cleaned hourly," Mae explains. "Wherever you go in the world, you can almost be guaranteed of a decent bathroom when you see the double arches. Even in Bali."

"Huh. Things I learn." I pull into the bus parking in the lot. "I'm going to check on Cisco. He doesn't like the winding roads."

"Want us to get him a happy meal without the burger or fries or drink? I think they have them with apples and carrots."

Zoe walks backward toward the building.

I'm touched she wants to buy a treat for Cisco. He's going to get spoiled by her.

"Nah, he's fine."

I open the trailer and make sure Cisco's okay. It's early enough in the day, the temperature's not too bad. Wearing his fly mask calms him. This one makes him look like a superhero with a blue outline around his eyes on a red background.

Yeah, forget the getting part, he's already a spoiled horse.

When the girls return, I'm leaning against the driver's side of the truck, happily checking out Zoe walking toward me. Her long legs are highlighted by the ripped jeans she's wearing. Beneath her thin T-shirt, I can see the slight bounce of her breasts with each step. Taller than Mae, Zoe's curvier than her shorter friend.

Dancing with her last night wasn't enough. I want to feel her naked body slide against mine as I explore her curves.

Behind my sunglasses, I let my gaze roam over Zoe, taking in all of her and committing it to memory. As they step closer, I bite the inside of my thumb, near the nail to stifle a grin threatening to spread across my face. Her beauty isn't based on makeup and clothes. It shines out of her, bright like the high altitude sun.

"Ready?" Zoe interrupts my thoughts.

"More than ready." For her? Definitely.

With a grin, I jog around the front and open the doors. Mae's nice, but I'm kind of wishing she wasn't here. Not going to leave her behind in a random parking lot, but I don't need a chaperone.

If I thought Zoe was hot before, the soft moans and happy sighs she makes while eating simple street food pushes me over an imaginary line. Sitting across from her, I stare as she takes a big bite of taco. I swallow my own groan when she licks a drop of crema from the corner of her mouth and then sucks more sauce off her fingers.

An hour ago I was resolved to take it slow and get to know her. Now I'm imagining her mouth on me.

"Excuse me." I clear my throat. "I'm going to get more hot sauce. Need anything?"

With a mouthful of food, Zoe just shakes her head no.

"Mas hot sauce, por favor," Mae says with a terrible Spanish accent.

Her humor breaks through a growing haze of lust. Evidently, I do need a chaperone.

Post tacos, Zoe wipes her mouth with a stack of napkins. "I feel like I've washed my face with guacamole. So worth it."

"Avocado facials are why we millennials are picked on for our financial status," Mae says, wadding her napkin into a ball and tossing it into the empty taco tray.

"That's not a real thing, is it?" I ask.

"The financial woes of millennials or our rampant love of avocados?" Mae asks.

"Both?"

Zoe steals one of my tortilla chips and dips it into the way too small cup of extra guacamole. "Apparently, we're not taking adulting seriously because we're obsessed with avocados."

"All of us?" I really am out of the loop if my entire generation is failing financially. Will I get booted from the club when they find out I'm actually good with money?

"Pretty much," Zoe says. "Aren't you on social media?"

"No."

Both women stare at me like I've announced I don't have electricity. Sometimes I don't, but that's not the point.

"How do you find out what's going on in the world?" Mae asks, stunned by my confession.

"I read the paper."

"Actual newspaper?"

"Online if I have Wi-Fi." Pulling my oversized iPhone from my back pocket, I wiggle it in front of Mae. "I have one of these fancy computer phones that let me get on the world wide web. And I know what Candy Crush is and that it's evil."

"Okay, grandpa." Zoe winks and then gives me an exaggerated thumbs-up.

"You're not the first to call me an old man. Thing is, I don't want to spend my life staring at a screen. What's the point of sitting at home watching other people living their best lives? Or at least pretending to. From what I've seen, most of what's online is exaggerated at the best and outright bullshit at the worst. No, thanks."

Behind her big sunglasses, it's impossible to read Zoe's eyes. As I study her, a small line forms between her brows and she gives a tiny nod. "Are all cowboys wise like you?"

For a reason I don't examine, her comment stings. When I speak, my tone is full of sarcasm. "Yeah, sure. All the time we spend riding the range gives us the chance for deep introspection and philosophizing about life."

"That's a real thing, isn't it? The cowboy philosopher? I swear I heard about a book or podcast for applying the cowboy way of life to everyday living," Mae says.

"Are you sure it wasn't a decluttering manifesto?" Zoe asks.

"Cowboy way of life? You mean get up at the ass crack of dawn, work and sweat all day doing hard physical labor, deal with actual shit on a daily basis, get paid nothing, and end most days smelling like horses on a good day, or shit on the bad ones?" I chuckle.

"Stop. You're ruining the glamorous image I have in my head." Zoe holds up her hands. "Stop right now. I need the fantasy."

This time it's Mae who snorts and mutters under her breath, "Whatever gets you off."

Interesting. Zoe has cowboy fantasies? I tuck that little bit of information away for later.

FOURTEEN

ZOE

WHEN MAE MAKES a comment about getting off on cowboys, I stomp on her foot beneath the picnic table. The woman doesn't even squirm as I apply more and more pressure. Her pain tolerance is remarkable.

"Are you playing footsies with me?" Justin asks. The foot under mine lifts and wiggles around.

My cheeks heat as I duck my head to peer under the table. Sure enough, my foot rests on top of his boot, not Mae's sneaker. Makes more sense. Still doesn't change my urge to crawl under the bench and hide.

"What if I was?" I laugh off my embarrassment.

He lifts a dark eyebrow and stares at me. I'm not sure if it's a challenge or he's waiting for me to confess.

As we stare at each other, he switches the positions of our feet, placing the tip of his boot on the toes of my shoe, pressing down. Only his boot makes contact with my shoe, but a little spark zings around in my chest before traveling south.

"Okay, I'm still here," Mae interrupts the staring contest.

My focus shifts to her and I mouth, *"Sorry."*

"I'm not sure what's going on below this table, but I swear

I saw a bubble form around the two of you." With her fingers, she sketches a heart in the air around our heads.

Justin laughs and swings his legs over the bench to get up. "We should probably get back on the road before Zoe challenges me to arm wrestle."

It's weird I mourn the contact with his boot.

We pile into the truck's cab. Even more than before, I'm conscious of the small space. Focused on the proximity of him, his soap and sweet hay scent filling the small space, I zone out as we drive back to town. This part of the ride flies by and soon we're passing the local airport.

"Where's your condo?" Justin asks.

"Huh?" I blink away my daydreams of open fields and full skin contact.

"Address? Or I can drop you on a corner if you want to keep it a secret." His voice softens with his offer.

"We know where you live, it's only fair you know where I do, too." I tell him the street and number.

I point out the condos on our left as he slows in front of the driveways. "We're here."

He nods. "Nice place."

"Thanks." My hand grips the door handle, but I don't open it. "We really appreciate the ride. We'd probably be still sitting in front of the hotel, starving."

"You're welcome." His voice is soft and only for me.

Mae coughs to get our attention. Finally, I open the door and when she hops down, she gives me a confused look. I scramble out behind her.

"Thank you!" I give him a cheery wave.

From behind me, Mae says through her laughter, "You already said that."

"Hey, we should go to Hick House together some time." Justin gives me that slow, sexy grin.

"She'd love to," Mae replies for me. I spin to give her a dirty look.

"Great." Justin agrees. "Enter your number in my phone."

He's already passing me his phone before I can think of a reason to say no.

I'm beginning to feel like I have three fairy godmothers and none of them can agree on what's best for me.

Mae's all about living in the moment.

Mara wants me to be adventurous, but only focus on myself.

Sage is the voice of reason, or at least, caution. She also knows me the best.

A girl could do with less advice. Even well-meaning and from the heart advice from amazing, strong women like them.

My heart flutters around in my chest every time I think about Justin leaning against his truck yesterday. All long legs and muscle, with the sexiest confident grin on this face, he's a pretty fine specimen of man. Objectively speaking.

It's too bad cowboy fantasies aren't going to pay my rent or help me figure out what I want to be when I grow up. Or even who I am now. Because somewhere in the last five years, I lost pieces of myself like missing socks. At first I didn't notice, or just assumed they were still around and would show back up eventually.

I've finally accepted I need to do something for me. Reclaim Zoe. My reality is I have a month squatting and dog sitting before I need a plan for what comes next.

So far this means listening to a bunch of empowering podcasts and watching YouTube videos about self-care and bullet journaling. The journals with all the pretty stickers and cheerful motivation are tempting.

The blank application for a month residency at Ashcroft Arts

Ranch in Snowmass stares back at me from my laptop screen.

Since grad school I've had the fantasy of being accepted for a month at the ranch. Four weeks of nothing but making art, twenty-four hour access to kilns, and a studio of my own. A little pocket of heaven for an artist.

My fingers tap away at the keys as I enter my biographic information. When I get to the personal essay section, my fingers stop and hover over the keys. My artist statement hasn't been updated since my MFA show. Hell, I've barely made anything new in over two years. Since moving here, I can count on one hand the times I've fired anything in a kiln. Sure I can blame focusing on my relationship with Neil and taking advantage of life in the mountains, but it's a sad excuse for fear.

Fear of failing.

Fear of selling out.

Fear of sucking.

Mara's question about wanting to be a massage therapist still rattles around in my head.

I don't want to make mugs and bowls for the rest of my life either. There's a difference between a potter and a ceramic artist. Not that the world at large cares.

There are a lot more uses for mugs and bowls than Japanese *kintsugi* inspired sculptures.

Receiving a fellowship at Ashcroft is a long shot for any artist. It's crazy to even apply, but if I'm not in the arena at all, I'll never have a chance to win.

I'm halfway to talking myself out of applying when I paste my statement and link to my MFA portfolio. I tell myself this is pointless as I enter my credit card information for the application fee. I'm clearly hopelessly delusional when I click submit.

Pretending I didn't just waste seventy-five dollars, I slam my laptop closed and toss it to the other end of the sectional.

"Well, that didn't just happen, so there's no point in worrying about it now," I tell Nell and Hunter, who are both asleep on their adjoining dog beds. Neither even twitches an ear at my declaration. "That's the right attitude. Nothing to see here. Nothing at all."

My application is for next year, but I added a note in my cover letter about taking a shorter residency if they have a cancellation for this season. If I'm already local, maybe they'll consider me above other candidates.

"Hopes. I have them." I peel myself off the sectional. "Now to figure out where I'm going to live when your parents come back."

Not only am I talking to the dogs, I'm doing it while they're asleep.

My phone rests on the counter, charging. I pick it up to double-check my massage appointments later today and see several texts alerts.

The first is from Justin. I skip it to read Mara's message.

Giddy up! I made a reservation for us to take riding lessons on Sunday. I'll pick you up at ten.

Why ride a horse when I could ride a cowboy?

I text her back with a thumb's up and a horse emoji.

My finger hovers over Justin's name. I can't even pretend I don't know it's him because the previous shows the first line, where he says it's him.

Hi, it's Justin. Cowboy taxi service.

I smile at his introduction. It's possible I'd grin over him texting me the weather report.

You, me, and some messy barbecue? I'm at the Snowmass rodeo tomorrow night and off on Thursday and Sunday. Let me know your schedule.

He's asking me out. I think.

If I'm going riding with Mara, I'm going to guess we'll be sore, and probably bruised by Sunday night.

Thursday is the day after tomorrow. He's not wasting any time in following up on his offer from yesterday. Asking me out with two days' notice probably breaks some rule about dating, but I've had it with following rules.

I like a man who knows what he wants, but can I handle a hot cowboy?

Inside my head, I hear my friends' voices. Because that's normal.

Sage says take things slow.

Mae says shave my legs and maybe get a bikini wax.

Mara says you only live once.

I type my response, erase it, and retype a new one. Staring at it, I start to overthink.

Like the application, I hit enter before I can talk myself out of it.

I'd love to see you on Thursday.

FIFTEEN

JUSTIN

WEDNESDAY NIGHT I scan the stands as we line up in formation during the National Anthem. Zoe never said she'd be here, but it doesn't stop me from looking for her dark hair among the rodeo crowd.

When I ride out of the gate after the introductions, Gentry waits for me and takes the reins as I dismount. "You ready for tonight?"

"Always am." I meet his eyes. "Prepared and focused."

"Heard you skipped training for a hike."

I ignore the edge of disappointment. "You know I wouldn't cut out on training if I didn't think I was ready."

"Never hurts to practice. You think Beethoven blew off playing the piano?"

"God, I hope so. You know my goals with competition. Do well, don't get hurt. I've never wanted to go on the national circuit. If I win, great. If I can walk away after a show, even better. Plus, I'm aging out. I'll be thirty soon. An old man."

Gentry glowers at me. "You could've been one of the greatest. Hall of Fame."

I see the ambition in his eyes. "You know fame is a four letter f-word, right? When have I ever had any desire to be famous? You've been with me from the beginning. Summers only. That was my agreement."

"Wasting talent is the worst," he mutters, giving me a disapproving shake of his head. "I should've stood up to your grandmother and never let you accept her deal. Part time rodeo, part time number cruncher isn't a full life."

"I disagree. I get the best of both. Spending my life chained to a desk, making money for other people would be worse."

Gentry pats my shoulder. "At least you came to your senses early about that."

"I don't know what I would've done without you." I hold out my hand to shake his. "Thank you."

He eyes me before gripping my hand in his gnarled, thick fingers. "Enough of this deep, soul searching talk. You better get yourself ready for the bronco ride."

Resting my hand on his shoulder, I chuckle at how quickly he cut off the conversation. Any mention of the life that could've been if I continued on a different path, and the man shuts it down. Sure, I gave up five years of riding full time for college. Twenty-three is late to join the circuit and I've come to terms with it.

I wonder how Gentry handles any real emotion. He's somewhere between my dad and grandfather's ages. They're men from a different generation. Men who could travel through life using silence, distance, whiskey, drugs—whatever they could to keep any emotion at bay.

No wonder some men feel nostalgic for the good old days. Cowboys. Westerns. Simpler times.

Never mind the violence, desperation, loneliness, alcoholism, poverty, and disease of the American West. The small pox. The genocide.

Good thing Gentry isn't a mind reader. If he knew where my thoughts had just wandered, he'd never speak to me again. Better off being the strong, silent type.

The evening ends with another win and more points toward the season's overall score. I accept the applause with a tip of my hat.

"Does winning ever get boring?" Dusty asks as we ride out of the arena.

"Never."

"Ever thought about giving the rest of us a shot at the number one spot?"

"I do. Every night we climb on our horses I think maybe it's the rodeo when one of you is going to show up and challenge me." I trot past him. "Maybe this weekend."

Over my laughter I can hear Dusty shouting, "You're a fucking arrogant asshole, Garrison."

Tossing him a look behind my shoulder, I reply, "Watch your language. This is a family show."

Once I have Cisco loaded in the trailer I realize none of the guys invited me out for drinks tonight.

Either I am an asshole, who no one wants to include, or they've finally picked up on the clue I'm not interested in cheap booze and random boobs.

Probably both are true.

Inside my truck's cab, I pull out my phone and check for messages.

When I see Zoe's name, my grin is bigger than the one I had when I won tonight. Let the rest of the guys spend the night getting shit-faced with the hopes of unmemorable sex.

I have a date with a funny, smart, and undeniably beautiful woman tomorrow night. A little rusty at dating, to be sure, I'm looking forward to spending the evening with her.

By Thursday afternoon, I'm antsy. Not nervous, more impatient.

A few more hours and I'll be picking up Zoe for our date.

To pass the time and keep out of everyone's space, I'm practicing roping with the calf dummy behind the horse barn. Gentry would tell me to set the damn thing up properly and practice with Cisco.

The thing is, Cisco doesn't need the extra work. Truth, neither do I.

Better than pacing around my cabin or annoying Tammy in the kitchen.

The dummy I'm using has a realistic calf head, which is creepier than fuck with its sad expression. My goal is always to beat my best time and win, not hurt the calf or Cisco.

Coil the rope, toss, and visualize it looping around the head.

Repeat.

The rope thunks on the metal time after time in a satisfying rhythm.

"Something troubling you?" Jeb strolls over and loosens the rope from the dummy.

"No." I grin at him in thanks.

"Are you sure? Tammy sent me out here." He scratches his chin with nails that need a cleaning and a trim.

"Tell her to mind her own business."

"She said you only use the dummy when you're upset about something. None of my business, but I don't want to get on her bad side. I'd probably die if I had to cook my own food."

"Starve, maybe. I bet you'd probably figure out how to drive yourself to the store and forage for food. Eventually." My rope loops around the dummy's head again.

Jeb tosses it back to me. "Suit yourself."

I expect him to walk away, but he leans against the fence, resting one boot on the lowest rung.

"Need something?" Looping the rope, I stare at him.

"Just watching."

I lift my eyebrows. "Did I ask for an audience?"

"Jesus, Justin. With the size of your ego, I'd figured you'd like an audience telling you how good you are."

"I already know. Don't you have work to do?" Nothing about me standing behind the barn says I want company.

"Nah, finished up my chores."

"And decided to hang around the kitchen?" A few pieces click into place and I chuckle. Tammy's staff is mostly younger women.

"The door was open and I heard laughter."

"You realize Tammy sent you to find me to get you out of her hair, right?" The woman knows how to manipulate people to get the results she needs.

Realization brightens his eyes. "Well, damn."

"Better smarten up around here, or you'll be doing all of Tammy's chores before you know it." Sweet, dumb Jeb.

Because I can, I swing the rope and encircle his shoulders with it. A gentle tug tightens the loop.

"Hey!" He wiggles around, trying to free himself.

Probably makes me an asshole, but I laugh at his struggle.

"What'd you do that for?"

"Wondered if I could. Turns out I can."

"You're a smug bastard." He loosens the rope enough it drops to the ground.

"And I'm your boss."

Grumbling, Jeb steps away from the fence. "I'll leave you to your bad mood."

His words make me chuckle. My mood hasn't been this good in months, maybe years. Guess I need to work on expressing my sunny disposition. I could start wearing unicorn T-shirts and get a smiley face button for my jean jacket.

"If you want, take off early for your day off tomorrow. You don't need to hang around here tonight." I try to make amends for being a jerk.

"Really?"

"It's good to get off the ranch every once in a while to remember there's a big, wild world out there. Go camping or something. Hiking's always a good idea."

"I was thinking of driving down valley and seeing some friends in Glenwood."

"Get out of here. Your friends will be happier to see you than I am. Go."

"Serious?" He finally gets the clue.

"Do I joke about time off?" I've got a board of spoiled trustees to answer to. Gotta keep this place running as a well-oiled operation. Or have them vote me out and then sell the land for overpriced second homes. My goal is to make sure that never happens in my lifetime.

"Thank you."

He can't see my smile as he runs to his cabin. Sure, I'm gruff, but I don't want the guys to hate me. No one wants a miserable work environment, including me.

Showered, shaved, and dressed in fresh jeans, a black shirt with the sleeves rolled, and a pair of boots, I brush a hand over my short hair and make sure I don't have toothpaste on my chin.

With a deep exhale, I pick some imaginary lint from my chest. "Ready."

This is the Hick House, not prom.

Then why are my palms damper than normal?

I lock the cabin door behind me, jiggling the handle to

make sure it's closed. Not that I think anyone's going to steal anything, but pranks are popular around the ranch.

I don't need to come home to shaving cream in my boots or cling wrap on the toilet. Both have happened to me before. There's a fake snake in a kitchen drawer for when I need to seek my revenge.

A wolf whistle greets me when I step down from the cabin's porch. Tammy's leaning out the screened door from the kitchen.

"You keeping something from me, Garrison?" she yells. A huge grin splits her face.

"Nothing you need to worry about." My lips curve into a happy smile.

"I know that look. You're going to tell me all about this woman at breakfast tomorrow morning." She leans back into the kitchen and says something over her shoulder I can't hear. "If you are back for breakfast."

A couple of the ranch hands coming back from the barns slow their pace to catch the show.

"I'll be sure to make an official announcement." I send an exaggerated glower in Tammy's direction and jerk my head toward our audience.

"Oh, please. We have a pool around here." Her warm grin balances my sour expression.

"For?" I stop walking and so do the guys.

"When you're going to get yourself a girlfriend." Tammy sounds way too happy about this nightmare.

"Who?"

Her eyes drift up, like she's counting in her head. "Pretty much everyone but you. Your grandmother called from Santa Fe to add her bet."

"Felecia Garrison doesn't believe in gambling." Crossing my arms, I glare at the young bucks, who are openly eavesdropping. "Don't you have somewhere else to be?"

They resume walking. In opposite directions. Like cockroaches scattering when the light is turned on.

"Maybe you should call your grandmother more often and you'd know. Nothing would make her happier than you falling in love, marrying, and giving her great-grandchildren."

"You're kidding about all this, right?" I ask as I pace closer to Tammy.

"Not even about the babies. Do you realize you've been snapping at the guys more than usual lately? I know you like to play the cranky loner, but you must've forgotten I've been around you for most of your life. I remember the sweet kid before you turned angry and cocky. I watched as you built that wall around yourself after Boyd died."

My spine goes iron straight at the thought of my father.

"See? I mention him and you go on high alert."

"I don't want to be him."

"Pretty sure you can't wake up one morning as a narcissist. He was born that way. Nothing your grandmother did stopped the runaway train of his life. Doesn't mean you're on the same track."

"Son of the son," I mumble.

"Bullcrap. I'm too old to buy that load of manure. I'm not going to let you go through life thinking you have some curse on your head."

"You sound pretty confident in yourself, Tammy."

"Well, Justin," she echoes me, "for one thing, you work your ass off keeping this ranch in the black. From what I saw, your dad was happy to suck it dry for his own selfish enjoyment."

She's right.

"Now if you stop acting like a prick, maybe a nice woman might give you more than a roll in the hay."

"Ouch." I cringe at her harsh truth.

"I married three of them, so that makes me a prick expert.

You act the part, but deep down, you know it ain't the real you."

"Wanting people to do their best isn't a bad thing."

"Never is, but there's different ways of going about pushing. Like a gentle nudge instead of shoving a guy's head in the toilet."

"Hey now, that was a punk prank when I was sixteen." I remember the incident when I first came here. "Got tired of being picked on for being from LA and needed to prove I belonged."

"Come here." She gestures for me to step closer. Brushing her hands over my shoulders and pecs, her face grows serious. "This ranch is yours. We all know who runs the show. And we're here to support you. Nothing more to prove."

Her words drop like stones in still water, rippling through me. "How'd you get so wise?"

"Same way you did. Experience." Her eyes crinkle when she looks up at me. "What's her name?"

A dog with a fresh bone, this one.

"Come on, bring a little joy into an old woman's life."

I scoff. "You're not old."

She tucks her chin and waits with her hands on her hips.

"Zoe. Her name is Zoe and she's from Chicago, but lives here."

"And?" I swear her toe taps with impatience.

"She's special. Funny, beautiful, and being around her puts a smile on my face."

"Apparently, so does talking about her." Tammy's eyes reflect delight.

Narrowing my eyes at her, I ask, "About this dating pool?"

"I have you down for late July. If you want to help a girl out."

"I'll be sure to keep that in mind." I lean down and give her a quick peck on the cheek.

"Save it for your Zoe." She waves me off. "Have fun tonight!"

The kitchen door slams behind her and I cringe at the sound.

The Easy Z ranch staff is a bunch of nosy gossips. Obviously, they don't have enough work to do if they have time to be filling out calendars about my social life.

Something I'll remind them of first thing tomorrow. Maybe I'll ring that damn triangle and tell them all to mind their business. And threaten to put everyone on rotation for mucking out the stalls, goat pen, and chicken coop.

SIXTEEN

ZOE

ONE OF THE most handsome men I've ever seen is standing on the other side of this door. When the doorbell dinged, I crept close as quietly as I could to peer through the peephole. Drinking in every gorgeous detail of Justin without getting caught is equivalent to eating dessert before dinner.

We all want to do it, but being polite, we resist the temptation.

Justin's one temptation I don't want to resist.

His dark shirt makes him look slightly dangerous. I make note of how long his fingers are as he sweeps them over his hair. It's short enough there isn't anything to run my fingers through, but I bet it would feel amazing brushing my skin. As he kissed his way south down my chest and stomach.

Whoa.

Waiting for me to answer the door, he turns his back and glances down the street. The movement allows me to get a gander of the caboose. His jeans fit his ass and strong thighs like they were custom cut for him. I wonder if cowboys use tailors.

His broad shoulders stretch the fabric of his shirt when he crosses his arms.

Justin is a patient man. He doesn't press the doorbell multiple times. Instead, he leans a shoulder against the entry's wall and crosses his ankles. Shifting his weight to one side, he's a picture of self-assured calm.

I wonder if I can snap a pic through the eyehole to send to Sage.

He pulls out his phone and checks the screen. I stand on my toes, hoping to check out his screen saver. The image a man chooses for his screen tells a lot about what matters to him.

Landon has a selfie of himself. Huge red flag.

My phone in my hand chirps with a message.

Loudly.

Like a duck.

Justin's head turns slightly. He keeps typing.

I fumble the phone when a second alert sounds. Right before I chuck it across the room, I notice the text preview.

Knock knock.

You say who's there.

Trying to stay silent, my laugh comes out a snort. There's no way he didn't hear that.

I pull open the door. "Hi. Sorry. Have you been waiting long?"

His eyes sweep down my simple black slip dress and bare legs to my lace-up sandals. The heel isn't high, but it's enough that it brings us closer in height. Being tall typically means flats for me so I don't tower over everyone like a giraffe.

When his focus returns to my face, the slow, sexy grin appears. I'm developing an addiction to seeing it. "Hi yourself."

"Want to come in? I need to find my phone and grab my bag." I swing the door wider for him to pass me.

He enters and stops a few feet away. "Nice place. Is your roommate home?"

I forgot about the white lie I told him before.

"No, it's just me." Not exactly clarification, but not really another fib. "And the dogs. But I put them in the bedroom so they wouldn't maul you with their excitement."

"You have dogs?"

"I'm dog sitting for some friends. Want to meet them?"

He's studying the room and doesn't respond right away. "Sure."

"You don't have to say yes."

He meets my eyes. "I'd love to."

"Okay, I'll gather the hounds. You might want to have a seat. They're less likely to bulldoze you if you're sitting." I give him a small smile.

In the bedroom, I unlatch the doors on the crates while giving both dogs a little pep talk.

"Don't lick his face. Or sniff his crotch. No trying to hump his leg."

I could give myself the same speech.

"Best behavior, you two." I open the bedroom door and both dogs scramble past me down the hall like they've been fired out of a cannon.

I jog after them, warning Justin, "Incoming!"

I'm too late. As I round the corner near the kitchen, I hear his muffled moan.

Both dogs are standing on the couch, flanking his sides. Nell licks his ear while Hunter is sniffing the top of Justin's head. He's hidden behind a wall of brown fur.

"I'm so sorry." I dash over to him. "Off. Down. Both of you. Listen. Sit."

My words have no impact.

"Enough." Justin's laughter fills the room. Hunter sits down and Nell jumps off the couch.

"How did you get them to listen?" I ask, finally able to see his face again.

"With dogs and horses, it's more about your tone than it is the words. They respect authority."

"No wonder they don't listen to me."

Justin gives me a curious look.

"I'll get them back in their crate now." Feeling a little embarrassed by the dogs, I click my tongue and say the one word they'll pay attention to. "Cookie."

Suddenly they both have eyes only for me. Grabbing two cookies from the jar on the counter, I lead them to the bedroom.

Upon returning to the living room, I notice Justin's beautiful black shirt is now striped with thin strands of dog fur.

"I'm so sorry. Let me grab a lint roller."

He stands and stares down at his shirt. "The one time I try to not be covered in horse hair. You should probably know I don't really do fancy."

I locate the roller in the junk drawer and begin rolling it up and down his chest. And abs. Up and down. Slowly down and back up. I can feel the ridges and valleys of muscle beneath.

"I think that spot's good." His hand on mine stills my movement.

"Sorry," I say, staring at his waist.

"No worries. I can do it myself."

Of course he can.

"I found your phone. It was buried behind some couch cushions." He points at the coffee table.

"Thanks. I'm always losing it."

"Ready?"

I grab the jean jacket I left on the barstool next to my clutch. "Definitely. I'm starved."

He meets me at the door. "Mind if we walk? It's a nice night."

"Sure." Outside, we stroll down the narrow sidewalks past charming cottages and Victorian mansions from Aspen's silver days. Even the tiniest house is worth millions in a billionaire's playground. I wonder if the crazy money makes a guy like Justin uncomfortable like it does me. I know he wins cash prizes from the rodeos and manages the ranch, but there's no way he could afford to live here.

Another thing we have in common.

With his hand on the curve of my lower back, Justin directs me to one of the patio tables outside the restaurant. The touch reminds me of when we danced together and the zings zoom through my body.

We're tucked in a corner. The umbrella is unnecessary for shade, but adds to the intimate feeling even though we're sitting feet away from Aspen's main street. Instead of sitting across from me, Justin sits to my left. Better for conversation and people watching.

The tiny blonde hostess does a not-so-subtle double-take as she gives Justin a menu. She barely glances at me and I have to grab the menu from her hand. When she stands there for longer than necessary, Justin and I meet eyes. He tilts his head in her direction and raises his eyebrows.

"We're all set," he says, keeping his tone friendly. "Unless you're waiting for our drink orders."

"Oh, your waiter will take those." She doesn't move to leave.

"Okay, well then." He stares up at her with a broad smile. "I think we're all set."

Still, she loiters by our table.

I clear my throat, and her eyes drift to mine. Bizarrely, she mouths, *"Oh em gee"* to me.

Now Justin and I both wear the same confused expression.

A busboy steps around the hostess, setting down glasses of ice water.

Justin scratches a spot behind his ear and chuckles softly.

Maybe I should throw my water at her. Snap her out of her Justin-induced stupor. I hope she never goes to the rodeo. There's no way she'd be able to handle him in chaps on the back of a horse. The hat might do her in at first sight.

We passed awkward two minutes ago.

A waiter joins our group, his smile fading as he notices the hostess statue.

"Becks? You working my table tonight?" His voice is teasing and his smile good natured.

Becks blinks a couple of times, returning to us from wherever she mentally traveled for the past few minutes. "Sorry. This is your server LJ."

"EJ."

A new level of awkward has been unlocked.

EJ earns a big tip by keeping his friendly grin. "Sorry to interrupt. Did Becks take your drink order? Or can I get you something from the bar?"

Three sets of eyes stare at Becks.

"You look familiar." She directs the comment to Justin.

EJ's eyes widen like she's broken the unspoken code in Aspen: never acknowledge a client or customer looks familiar for fear they might be famous.

Last ski season I had a massage appointment I swear was a former child star of a super popular wizard franchise. He'd booked under another name, and even though I'm positive it was him, I had to call him Bob and pretend he wasn't famous. Of course, some celebrities need the attention. And they'll announce it upon arrival.

Justin is rodeo famous, but he's also a local.

"Fan of the rodeo?" he asks.

"Never been," she replies, staring at him.

"Must be the shaved hair." He self-consciously brushes his hand over his head.

"I'll figure it out," Becks says as she finally wanders back to the host stand.

"Sorry about that. She's new." EJ drops two paper coasters on the table. "Drinks on me."

We both order beers from the draft list before EJ promptly leaves. From my seat, I watch him walk over to Becks and speak to her.

"Well, that was . . ." Justin leaves the rest of the sentence blank for me to fill.

"Awkward?"

"Odd?"

"Peculiar?"

"Unexpected?"

"Flattering?"

"Uncomfortable?"

EJ returns with our beers and asks if we're ready to order.

Neither of us has looked at the menu, but I get the same thing every time. "Can I get a Pig salad, with beef, no egg. Please."

"Salad?" Justin's jaw drops. "At the best barbecue joint in the area?"

"Calculated move. Based on the assumption you're going to get ribs."

"You plan on stealing my meat?" A teasing smile plays at the corner of his mouth. "Pretty forward."

EJ remains quiet.

Justin orders. "Combo two. Better make it a full rack if someone thinks I'm going to share."

EJ repeats our order, takes our ignored menus, and disappears.

"Sorry if I overstepped. Guess I'm used to sharing."

"With your other dates?'

Crap. I've waded into ex-boyfriend conversation.

I laugh it off. "No, my best friend dates a rugby player. He always orders enough food for a squad. If we're quick we can steal from his plate before he growls at us."

Justin laughs with me. "I promise I won't growl at you."

When our food arrives, Justin curls his arm around his huge platter of ribs and pulled pork, and snarls at me.

Laughter bursts out of me. "Message received."

"What happened to your dainty girl salad?" He points at the mound of brisket burying the lettuce beneath it on my plate.

"Ratio seems about right to me."

His eyes hold amusement as I stab a chunk of tender meat and bite into it.

Without prompting from me, he cuts off a couple of ribs and slides them onto my bread plate next to my garlic toast.

"You're a true gentleman, Justin Garrison."

"Why, thank you, Miss Zoe." He dips an imaginary hat brim. "I aim to please."

In all things probably.

I moan when the combination of sweet sauce and savory meat hits my tongue as I bite into the rib.

"Excuse me. Sorry to interrupt, but I remember where I know you from." Becks is back.

With the end of the rib in my mouth, I stare at Justin.

He wipes his sauce-sticky fingers on one of the napkins in the pile, but doesn't speak.

Maybe they used to date? He probably has pining and broken-hearted women scattered around the western states.

"You're a Garrison, right?"

He nods, eyes wary and apologetic when they meet mine. "I am. You've probably seen me at the Snowmass Rodeo."

"No, but maybe I will. I recognized you from the tabloids."

I lift my eyebrows. Why would a local cowboy be in any tabloid?

"All that's in the past now." Shifting in his seat, he drops his napkin on the table.

EJ appears again. "How's your food?"

He angles his body and blocks Becks, who gets the clue and walks away. "Sorry about her. Is she bothering you?"

"No, it's fine. Thanks for the intervention."

"I'll make sure you're left in peace for the rest of the meal. Dessert's on the house."

I finally pull the rib from my mouth, having forgotten I've been sucking on it the entire time. Things have gone from awkward to bizarre. Who is Justin?

"I'm sorry about that. Wow." He uses a fresh napkin to wipe the corners of his mouth.

I set the rib down. "What was that about?"

His dark eyes study me.

In turn, I stare at his thick lashes and the gentle arch of his eyebrows. The cut on his lip has disappeared. Freshly shaved, his jaw is all sharp angles above the strong cords of his neck and Adam's apple.

"My grandfather was an actor." He picks up another rib and bites into it.

Nonchalantly, I nod and stab my salad like having a famous relative is no big deal. As I flip through the Hollywood trivia in my head for a resemblance or someone named Garrison, I casually ask, "Anyone I've heard of?"

"Really? Garrison? Cowboy?" His voice holds a slight edge of something that could be disbelief.

I press my lips together and shake my head. I'm still shaking it when the name clicks.

"Hold on . . . your grandfather is Rexland Garrison?" I fail to keep the starstruck awe from my voice. I know I've failed because Justin's eyebrows lower and his lips flatten. It happens and disappears in a blink.

The only reason I recognize the name is from my Netflix binge. "Country Rex" Garrison has his own subsection under Westerns. Because he made like a hundred of them in the sixties and seventies.

"Yes, Rexland is my dad's father." His voice remains flat.

"So that means you're . . ."

"Boyd Garrison's son."

"Hollywood royalty," I whisper like we're in church or having tea with the Queen of England.

"There's no such thing. Hollywood isn't a kingdom. It's all smoke and figments of our collective imagination. My grandfather bought the land here to create something real in his life. Ironic he used the money he made playing pretend to do it."

"He's a legend."

"Was. He's been dead for fifteen years."

"I guess he made an impression on you."

Justin nods, but doesn't appear happy. "Growing up I had zero desire to go into the family business or turn into the next legacy brat with a sex tape. My mother packed us up and moved here when I was sixteen. I resented her, the move, the ranch . . . pretty much everything. I threatened to take her to court for emancipation."

If I remember correctly, his dad lived in LA. His parties were both infamous and notorious, if the tabloids are to be believed. Another Garrison family fact slams into my brain. Ten years ago, his father died in the bed of a studio head, with the guy's wife beside him. *El Scandalo* was one of the more memorable headlines.

"From the look on your face, I'm guessing you know all about my dear old dad. Whatever you think you know, the reality is exponentially worse. The Garrison name kept a lot of things out of the press, even when a single photo could bankroll a tabloid for a year. Felecia Garrison is formidable when it comes to protecting who and what she loves."

"I'm not judging. Processing." I can't imagine being part of a famous family and having my dad die when I was a teenager.

He lifts his eyebrows in question. "Not the simple cowpoke you once imagined? My family comes with enough baggage to fill a covered wagon. Sorry to ruin the fantasy for you."

The genuine sadness in his voice pierces my heart. "If we're sharing secrets, I never had a cowboy fantasy until the first night at the rodeo when I saw you."

The sadness in his eyes disappears as he smiles. "Really? Tell me all about this fantasy."

He reaches across the small table to take my hand. His thumb traces over my thumb. I lean into his touch, letting it zing through my body before settling between my legs.

And he's only touching my hand.

"What are you thinking?" he asks.

I flip back to his family and Beck's comment. "You've been in the tabloids? Recently?"

"Thinking of going to the market later and scoping out all the dirt on me?"

"Never." I pick up another rib and jab it in the air in his general direction. "One thing you should know about me, I don't care about the past."

He nods. "Good. Neither do I."

"Good." I bite into the meat.

"To answer your question. Yes and no."

"Really?"

"Nothing too exciting or recent. Red carpet at the Golden Globes when my grandfather received a lifetime achievement award. The foreign press, especially the Italians, loved Rex. All those Spaghetti Westerns bankrolled the ranch."

"But you were a kid when your grandfather was honored." I know because I have a vague memory of that award show. "I doubt Becks has that good of a memory."

"There've been few random pictures with my sisters. And a couple of years ago there was an issue of *People* about Hollywood legacy families. They sent a photographer to the ranch. I'm sure you can find it online easily enough." A thin line forms between his thick eyebrows.

The thought is tempting for a moment until I reverse our roles. Do I want Justin searching my Internet footprint? What would he find? Sadly, nothing of interest.

"You don't come across as someone interested in being famous."

Pausing to take a sip of beer, he meets my gaze. "I can't imagine anything worse than being famous for my parentage. There's nothing worse than children of the famous running around and acting like they're important. For what? Winning a genetic lottery? No, thank you." Humor makes the corners of his eyes crinkle. "Unless it's the cover of *Rodeo Man*. And I can go shirtless."

Dead.

Stick a fork in me, I'm done.

The first thing I'm going to do when I get back to Sage's is look for shirtless pictures of him. Because my imagination is good, but I'm sure the reality is so much better.

"Would you autograph my copy?" I tease back.

"I'll even buy you a frame so you can put it on your nightstand."

"I'm going to need a poster size print."

Chuckling, he licks a drop of sauce off the side of his thumb. I lose the ability to focus on anything but the tip of his tongue sliding past his full lips and gently sweeping his skin.

Needing a moment, I focus on jabbing lettuce leaves onto my fork.

He continues talking like I'm not over here melting into

a pile of goo. "It's easy to disappear from the spotlight when so many others are desperate to hog the light. Sure, over the years I've had people show up at the ranch asking questions about the Garrison legacy. My life goal has been to be boring. Boring doesn't sell papers."

"What about the rodeos?"

"Sometimes the fun facts of my lineage get added to my introduction, but I ask to keep the focus on me and my accomplishments. Gentry's good about making sure Buzz Garrison is the star, not who my family is."

"Gentry?"

"He's my mentor and trainer. I guess he's like a manager, if we were in the big time. You've probably seen him lurking around the rodeo. Huge silver mustache and resting cranky face?" Justin wiggles his fingers in front of his upper lip.

"You've described a human walrus." I mimic his gesture.

I thought I'd heard Justin laugh before, but he's been holding back. His whole face lights up as he tips his head backward with laughter. After a moment, he inhales a deep breath and says, "I'm going to tell him that just to piss him off."

I toss a napkin at him, which he easily catches. "Please don't make enemies on my behalf."

"Gentry needs the reality check." Justin grins at me.

I smile back.

"Enough about me. I hate talking about myself. Nothing more boring than hearing me droning on and on. And on." He dips his chin and looks up at me. "What about you?"

His words make me chuckle. "There's not a lot about me to tell. Biographic details you know. Moved here because my best friend did. Working as a massage therapist to pay the man."

"What do you do when you're not working? Or focused on paying bills?"

"Apparently take long walks over mountains and hang out

at rodeos."

"Besides those two things." He shifts his position so he's resting his forearms on the table, which brings him closer to me. I catch the scent of leather and sandalwood from his skin.

"I'm an artist." I clear my throat. "I have my MFA."

"Impressive. What do you make?" He sounds genuinely interested.

"Nothing lately. If you haven't noticed, this town is expensive. I work as much as I can."

"Then move somewhere cheaper."

"I can't. I love it here."

He rolls his lips together and nods. "I know the feeling."

How? I want to ask. If he's one of the Garrisons, he's probably sitting on a trust. Never lived off of Ramen to stretch a paycheck. Instead, I say the thing we all say about living high in the mountains.

"It's magical here. Easy to forget the rest of the world exists."

"What do you want to forget?" His voice is soft. "Or who?"

I've avoided all mention of Neil and the breakup until now. First rule of first dates is to not mention exes and I'm not about to break it.

"I miss having a studio and time to turn thoughts into objects. If I can figure out a way to do that here, then I'm never leaving." Not exactly an answer to his question, but it's the truth.

Rubbing his thumb along the corner of his mouth, he stares at me. "Sounds simple enough."

"I applied to be a resident at Ashcroft next summer. The arts ranch in Snowmass?"

"I know it." The line forms between his brows for a second and then disappears.

"If I get in, I'll get room and board along with a studio of my own, twenty-four seven access to kilns. It's basically my idea of heaven."

"Why aren't you there this summer?"

"I missed the application deadline last year." Because Neil didn't want me to commit to something that could interfere with summer travel plans. That turned out well. "It's highly competitive. Doubtful I'll get a spot, but I'll never find out if I don't try."

"That sounds like the first time I got on a bull in competition."

"Ceramics are less likely to break my ribs."

"True. I guess I get used to always having something on my body hurting or aching."

The image of him lying on the dirt flashes in my mind, making my breath hitch. "What about you? You said you don't want to go on the national circuit. Why?"

"Mostly because I hate being away from home. Makes me a cranky bastard. Or more of one, if you ask anyone who knows me."

"Gentry mentor you in that area, too?"

His neat rows of white teeth appear when he smiles. "Gentry's going to love you."

"Why's that?"

"He loves strong, smart women."

I hope he's not the only one, because it would be ridiculously easy to fall in love with this cowboy.

SEVENTEEN

JUSTIN

THIS DATE HAS jumped the rails a few times tonight and we're still eating dinner.

Being sideswiped by Becks and her nosiness threw me off. I can't remember the last time someone bothered to ask me about my famous family. Not randomly in public, anyway.

A decade later, and we're still picking up the pieces from my father's messy exit. Mom spends a lot of time in her house outside of Santa Fe. My sisters in California aren't directly tied to Hollywood or anything to stir up the memory of Boyd or Rex. My own damn fault for living and breathing the ranch and rodeo.

When Zoe mentions applying to Ashcroft, I focus on keeping my features neutral.

No reason a cowboy, even a Garrison legacy, would know much about an arts and crafts center.

Or be on the board.

Not even if he's the grandson of one of the founders.

My grandmother might've been the heart and willpower to keep our ranch going for all those decades, but Felecia Garrison is also a lover of the arts and dabbles in painting.

Named for a nearby ghost town, Ashcroft's the favorite darling of my grandmother. While she doesn't handpick the artists anymore, she does wield influence over the rest of the board.

My role is fiduciary, but I could make a phone call or two.

The trouble is all final decisions are merit based and in a blind portfolio review. No biographic information is allowed in the selection process. Of course someone on staff knows.

I ask myself if the roles were reversed, would I want her to pull strings? No, I'd want to earn the spot on my own.

While I'm mentally meddling in her future, Zoe tries to bring the conversation back to me.

I'm genuinely not interested in talking about myself. Instead, I tell her about the Easy Z.

"It's a little oasis around here. Not much has changed since it was purchased in the fifties. Same log cabins and central dining hall."

"Sounds charming."

"You should come up this weekend and I'll give you the tour."

Her full lips press together in a frown. "I'd love to, but I'm working on Saturday and have plans with a friend on Sunday."

"Then we'll figure out another time. You should come when we're having a cookout and bonfire. We even have a couple of guys who sing old country songs and play the fiddle."

A smile softens her face. "You're selling the whole package."

"I'm happy to indulge someone's fantasy." My words are deliberately vague, and when I see her blush, I know she's thinking of her cowboy fantasy statement from earlier. Good, because I can't stop thinking about her words.

The busboy clears our plates and Zoe asks for a to-go box. I'm not sure why she looks sheepish asking, but she keeps giving excuses about getting a doggie bag.

"Don't feed the bones to the dogs. They can shatter and

be dangerous."

"It's not really for the dogs. More like lunch tomorrow."

She lives in a two million dollar condo, but saves leftovers for the next day? Maybe that's how she can afford to live in the heart of Aspen's west end. Or her mystery roommate makes bank. Earlier, while I waited for her to crate the dogs, I took a quick inventory of the space. Expensive furniture, lots of home accessories and stylish clutter, but nothing personal. No framed family or group friend photos. Nothing to give me an insight into Zoe.

"Do you have any of your work at the condo? I'd love to see what you make." My words are genuine. Plus, I'm not ready to end the evening just yet.

"Um, a few things. Most of it's in boxes. Or at my parent's house." Ducking her head, she plays with the sleeve on her jacket.

"If it makes you uncomfortable, show me another time." I touch the back of her hand, gently resting mine over hers and stilling her fidgeting. "Hey."

She meets my eyes.

"I want to get to know you. All of you. Not just the gorgeous, sexy, funny part you've already shown me."

"You can't say things like that," she whispers.

"Why? If they're true?"

"Because I'll believe you."

"And this is a problem because?" I lace my fingers with hers and bring our joined hands to my thigh.

"If I tell you, it'll be breaking rule number one for dating."

"You're married?"

"Lord, no." She inhales a deep breath. "Recent breakup."

My mood pops like a balloon. "How recent are we talking?"

"A couple of months, but we were together a long time."

I nod, but don't comment.

"It's over. So over. Taylor Swift is writing a new break-up song about how over we are." Her smile is forced.

"Now the cowboy fantasy makes sense. Summer. Rodeo. Rebound fling." Classic.

And now I sound like the cranky bastard people think I am.

Her eyes widen as she shakes her head. "Most of that's wrong. But it's why I left the rodeo the other night. You were flirting with me and I freaked out. I didn't expect you to even talk to me. You were safe because you were a fantasy."

"I need to practice my skills then." I drop her hand as our waiter gives me the bill folder. Flipping it open, I check the math and slip in my credit card.

"You didn't have to buy dinner. I'm happy to split it."

This date has turned into one of those pumpkin catapults. Full of hope and beauty as the orange squash sails through the air, but the ending is a mess.

"I asked you out. I'm a little old fashioned when it comes to dating. And I definitely don't expect anything to happen because I paid." My defenses flair into rudeness.

She blinks her thick, dark lashes at me as pink tinges the whites of her eyes. *Please don't cry in public.* There's nothing worse than a woman crying, except in public and from my jerky behavior.

"I'm sorry. That was a completely inappropriate comment. On many levels."

"I didn't mean to sound ungrate—" she whispers.

I interrupt her. "Do not apologize. I'm the asshole."

"My ex used to make comments about money. He made a lot more money than I do and never let me forget we weren't financial equals."

He sounds like a jerk and now I feel like an even bigger asshole. "Sounds like you did the right thing getting rid of him. A man should never try to make you feel less. If a man loves a woman, he wants the best for her and her happiness above all, including his own."

"Did I mention I'm single now?" Brushing a lock of hair out of her face, she gives me a shy smile.

I'm not sure how we jumped the rails, but I'm glad she's not walking out of here and not looking back. "Shall we go?"

With a nod, she stands. "Thanks for dinner."

"My pleasure." I mean it even if I want to erase the last few minutes.

This time when we walk down the sidewalk, I link our hands together. Her fingers twine between mine and return the pressure.

"I can't remember the last time I held hands." She glances down at where our skin touches.

I give her a small smile. "I'm beginning to question your taste in previous boyfriends."

"So am I," she says, softly. "Believe me, so am I."

We're quiet on the walk, lost in our own heads. I'm surprised when we arrive at her condo.

"Do you want to come in? Or I can grab the dogs and we can continue our walk?" She sounds nervous.

"Why not both? I'll come in and then we'll walk the dogs."

"Great." She swings her hands between us as she steps toward the door.

I should probably wait until the official end of our evening, but I don't want to. When she reaches the first step, I gently tug on her hand and stop. Now we're the same height when she turns her head to face me.

"Change your mind?" she asks, scanning my face.

"No. Made it up, in fact."

With the hand not holding hers, I slowly touch her neck, dragging my thumb along her chin. Only a few inches separate us, but they're still too many and she's not close enough.

I release her hand and slip my arm around her lower back, bringing her even closer. Her breath brushes my cheek. Her eyes flutter close as I lightly press my lips to hers.

There's nothing hurried or rushed about this kiss. No expectations or baggage. It's pure and perfect. Like all good firsts should be.

Her lips are soft and full, and I don't bother trying to keep this chaste. Not when her hands coil around my shoulders and her fingers stroke my hair in a slow rhythm.

She opens her mouth, an invitation I accept as I sweep my tongue over hers. A soft moan escapes the space between our lips and I'm not sure if it came from her or me. Or both of us.

Her tongue finds mine and I let her explore a moment before taking control again. With my hand on her cheek, I angle her head, wanting . . . no, needing, to deepen this kiss.

Using her hands, she encourages me to take the final step to bring us on to the same level. I don't stop there, instead backing her up until she's against the wall of the entry. Sliding my knee between her legs, I shift her thigh to my hip. It would be so easy to lift her dress and feel her bare skin under my palm, but I'm trying to be a gentleman.

Her nails scrape my scalp as she slowly grinds against my leg.

So much for a polite, early goodnight kiss.

A car drives down the street, the headlights sweeping away the shadows creating a sense of privacy.

I establish a sliver of space between our lips. "We should probably walk the dogs?"

"Huh? I don't have any dogs." She tries to recapture my mouth.

"Hunter and Nell? You're dog sitting?

Slowly, she blinks at me. "Oh, right."

"Or we could spend the rest of the night kissing on the steps." I demonstrate this option by pressing my lips to hers again.

"Mmm, I like option two." She kisses me back, her hands sneaking into the rear pockets of my jeans. When she squeezes my ass, I stop trying to put the brakes on this.

After another minute of making out, I groan with some deep restraint that decides to show up. "We should walk the dogs. I'm trying to be a gentleman and I've already blown the goodnight kiss."

Leaning away, I can see her lips are swollen and deeper rose from my mouth. Her cheeks flush and her eyes are glassy. She looks thoroughly turned on. And I'm going to walk away in order to keep my promise to get to know her before I get her naked.

EIGHTEEN

ZOE

THREE DAYS LATER, I'm still spinning from Justin's good-night kiss.

Mother of pearl buttons, the man can kiss.

I'd worried he'd be all about speed and quick moves the way he is in the rodeo.

Nope.

Justin's kisses are slow and deliberate. Like he's thought about, planned for it, and practiced long and hard.

Oh, yeah. That too. Although I'm not surprised. Not after watching him in those chaps and Wranglers.

Pretty amazing he doesn't walk bow-legged.

Being the gentleman he is, he waited outside for me to collect the dogs and their leashes. Smart man probably knew my restraint was as thin as the oxygen around here.

I should've cancelled plans with Mara and hung out with Justin today. I've thought about it. I can go horseback riding with her some other time. This is his last day off for more than a week and he's going to be out of town every night but Wednesday.

Did I ditch my friend for a hot cowboy? No.

Instead, I'm dressed in black jeans and tall brown boots with Mae's chambray shirt over a white T-shirt. It's the horsiest outfit in my closet. These are my least favorite jeans, so if I have to burn them after today, I'm okay with that.

Yeah, I don't have high hopes for me on the back of a horse.

Mara picks me up in her sensible CRV. In the backseat she has a bag of apples and carrots.

"Did you bring us snacks?" I ask, reaching for an apple.

"Those aren't for you. They're bribes."

"For who?"

"The horses. I want my horse to like me, so she doesn't try to kill me. I figured I'd buy her affection with treats. Like I do with the cats."

"Those boys have murder in their hearts. No way a few kitty treats would stand between you and death."

"Aww, they can be sweet."

Notice she doesn't deny the hearts full of killing wishes.

"Are you willing to share with me? What if my horse gets jealous and hates me?"

"Guess you should've planned ahead and brought some sugar cubes." She follows the rotary around to the left, the direction not heading back to Snowmass.

"You and Neil obviously fell into a comfortable rut. Now's your chance to shake things up. Do stuff that you wouldn't normally do. What scares you? Do that. Unless it involves something that might actually kill you. You don't have to go crazy."

Allowing her words to settle, I steal an apple from the backseat. My own heart squeezes with the truth of her words. "What do you recommend, oh wise one?"

"Say yes. When a new opportunity presents itself, say yes. Do things you've never done before."

"Like horseback riding?"

Her lips press into a firm line. "Sure."

"Get us a pair of stallions." Her boyfriend is hot, but my thoughts are of Justin.

"Hell no, there's no way I'm riding a stallion. I'm only agreeing if the horse is old and arthritic."

Tilting my head, I give her a sympathetic smile. "We might have to fight each other for the oldest and slowest horse. I've never been riding before."

"You told the cowboy it's been a while."

"I stretched the truth. I've never been. Unless a carousel horse counts."

Her eyes widen. "I fell off a merry-go-round once. Reaching for the brass ring, I lost my balance and slid off the side. The ride had to be stopped and everyone complained. I think a few kids even booed."

"Wait, this is why you don't like horses?" I have to lean against the door to stare at her fully enough to express my shock.

"First of many." Her voice is serious.

"You know those aren't real horses, right? Neither are the pony rides outside grocery stores."

"Shut up."

"Maybe we can find you a little pony to ride. Or even better, an ass. I want a unicorn with a rainbow horn and sparkles." It's Aspen, anything is possible.

Mara nods in agreement. "I'm only riding a unicorn."

As we pass Aspen Highlands and begin winding up in elevation, I ask, "Where exactly are we taking these riding lessons?"

She grins, pleased with her choice. "The Easy Z! When I saw the name, I took it as a good omen."

"Turn the car around. Or pull over so I can throw myself out. You don't have to stop. Just slow down so I don't break anything major." I grip the door handle.

I feel the car slow as she brakes.

My eyes widen as I think she's taking me seriously. "I wasn't serious about leaping from a moving vehicle."

"Oh no. What's wrong with the Easy Z? Do they abuse their animals?"

Ever since Mara visited the local dog sled kennel earlier this year to make sure the dogs are well cared for, she's on a personal campaign to protect all the four-legged residents in the valley. The woman has a huge heart when it comes to animals.

"Justin runs the ranch."

She glances at me. "Who's that?"

"Hot cowboy. Belt Buckle." My stomach churns with nerves.

"Ooh," she whispers.

"We had a date on Thursday."

"It didn't go well?" She frowns with sympathy.

"A little rocky at times, but overall amazing."

"Then why aren't you excited about seeing him?"

"I am, but I don't want him to think I'm a stalker by showing up randomly where he lives." Or randomly being at a rodeo out of town. Or running into him on a trail.

"Not random. We have a reservation for two lessons. He probably won't even be around. I doubt Colorado's Cowboy of the Year gives beginner riding lessons."

She makes a good point. My anxiety eases a little as we approach the beginning of the ranch's fence.

We can probably have our lesson, live to tell about it, and leave without Justin ever knowing I was here. It's a solid, realistic plan.

By the time we pull into the dirt and gravel parking area, I'm convinced Justin will never know I've been here.

Still, I glance at the log cabins scattered among the thin pine trees, wondering which one is his.

We find the sign for the office and follow a short path leading toward the barns. Mara stops to say good morning to three pygmy goats and a pair of alpacas. For a woman who lives above goats and other animals, she's pretty excited to meet some new animals.

A young blond guy in worn jeans and a green plaid shirt comes flying out of the office, screen door slamming behind him. Unfortunately, he doesn't see us and slams into me, sending us both sprawling. I land on my ass and he tumbles over me before catching himself on his hands. We look like we're playing an impromptu game of Twister, without the mat. Half on top of me, his legs arch over mine.

"Don't slam the damn screen doors," a woman's voice yells from across the compound.

"Shit, shit, and shit." Cowboy pushes off his hands and stands, scooping up his straw hat from the ground. "I'm so sorry, ma'am."

Brushing off his palms on his jeans, he extends a hand to help me up. I accept the gesture and stand.

"For knocking me down or calling me ma'am?" I ask.

Mara giggles.

His cheeks flush. "Both? I'm sorry. Are you okay, miss?"

"I think so." Sweeping my hands over my ass and hips, I check for bruises. My tailbone is a little tender, but I'll live.

"Are you here for the riding lesson?" he asks

"We are. Two beginners under the name Keeley," Mara replies.

If possible, the ruddy color on his cheeks deepens.

"I'm your instructor. Jeb." He extends his hand. "I was just running back to my cabin to grab some gum before we started."

Gum? Why exactly does he need fresh breath for a riding lesson?

"I have some in my bag." Mara roots around in her bag and pulls out a packet. "Never leave home without it."

Jeb takes two pieces and I wonder how he's going to speak

around the wad of gum.

I try to catch Mara's attention. Jeb's weird. Cute, but he called me ma'am. *Do I look like a ma'am? Maybe I do.*

"Want to meet your horses?" Jeb gives us a friendly grin. Evidently, he's already moved on from our awkward first encounter.

"Shouldn't we start with the basics? Maybe work with a dummy horse? Or a saddle on a stump?" Mara twists a curl around her finger. "Not sure I'm ready for real horses yet."

Jeb studies her and then me. "The reservation didn't mention you're afraid of horses."

"Not afraid. I have a deep respect for them. From afar." Mara points to the parking lot.

"Maybe pretend we've never met a horse before and start there?" I suggest.

Jeb nods. "Um, sure."

"We brought treats." Mara lifts the canvas tote. "Apples and carrots because I wasn't sure what they'd like."

"The horses?" Jeb's confident smile wavers.

"I tried to eat an apple on the way here and got my hand slapped. If you want one, I can create a distraction," I say, stepping away from Mara.

"Okay then." Jeb rubs his hands together and then claps once. "Maybe we'll begin with introducing the tack."

We follow him into a room in the barn filled with horse equipment. Ropes, reins, pads, blankets, bits, saddles, and harnesses line the room. One wall has a row of hooks with what appear to be whips.

"No chains?" I ask.

Mara elbows me in the side.

"What?" I whisper. "Come one, we saw that movie together. No way your mind didn't go to the red room, too."

Jeb's pretending he's talking to children as he performs a

simple show and tell about each item.

"Are we in charge of dressing our horses?" Mara asks.

"No, they're tacked and ready for you."

"Great!" Mara gives him a thumbs-up.

"How about we go over to the ring and you can check out our group riding class?" He picks up two helmets off the shelf and hand them to us.

We agree, and he leads us over to a fence surrounding a dirt riding ring. On the way over, I notice a calf dummy and my mind immediately conjures images of Justin with a rope in his hand. Not paying attention to my footing because I'm having dirty thoughts, I misstep and trip on air.

Okay, focus, Zoe.

Inside the fencing, a group of kids in helmets confidently steer their horses around the circle. In the middle, a woman in a cowboy hat and an outfit similar to Jeb's shouts instructions and praise.

"How long have they been riding?" I ask.

"About a month."

"Are you kidding? Look how fast they're going!" Mara's voice shakes with nerves.

"You'd be surprised how quickly you'll learn," Jeb says, his confident smile returning.

She presses her lips together. "We'll see."

"Ready to get in the saddle?" he asks.

Mara and I stare at each other. I shrug.

Jeb fidgets with his cuffs. "I won't force you. How about we meet them and you can decide then?"

In contrast to the junior equestrians, we're two nervous old nellies.

Reluctantly we agree and trail behind him to a smaller ring holding two horses.

"Meet Dolly and Loretta, the sweetest horses on the ranch."

Jeb swings his arm in a broad arc, in case we missed the large brown beasts with black manes.

Mara and I both wave at the horses.

They turn and whinny at us, loping over to the fence where we stand. They don't stop until they can hang their heads over the top rung, sniffing and studying us.

I take a giant step back and feel Mara move behind me.

"Might be a good time for those treats," Jeb says with a laugh, petting the nose of one of the horses.

Taking a carrot from the bag, I hold it out like Justin taught me. Soft velvet brushes my palm as one of the horses eats from my hand.

"Dolly likes you."

I glance at Jeb who is focused on helping Mara.

"How'd you know carrots are her favorites?" a familiar deep voice asks from my other side.

Leaning on the fence, Justin grins at me. "Can't say I'm not a little jealous you came to my ranch to see Dolly and not me."

"I . . ."

He steps closer, laying a hand on Dolly's neck. I can feel his body heat and smell his fresh scent. Beneath the typical sandalwood and cut grass is a salty layer of sweat.

I take in his appearance and notice the front of his T-shirt is dirty. His faded jeans are ripped at the knee and covered in dirt. Instead of a cowboy hat, he's wearing a faded John Deere green baseball cap.

"I'm here to take a riding lesson." I finally find my words. "I swear I'm not stalking you."

"We do seem to be running into each other a lot this summer." He grins at me. "If you want someone to teach you to ride, all you have to do was ask. I'd be more than happy to give you a private lesson."

"It was Mara's idea." I cast a glance at Jeb

At the sound of her name, she turns and finally notices the hot cowboy standing next to me. "You're BB."

Justin's grin doesn't fall, but his eyes shift to me. "BB? B for Buzz?"

"Belt Buckle," she explains. "I'm Mara."

Jeb laughs into his shoulder.

"You call me BB one time and you'll be looking for work on another ranch," Justin tells him, his voice all business.

"Gotcha, boss." Jeb tips his hat.

"If this is a riding lesson, what are you all doing on this side of the fence?"

"Getting acquainted with the horses," Mara says.

Justin lifts his eyebrows in question.

I nod at Mara's words. "We're a little nervous. Do you have any ponies around here? Or rocking horses?"

"Friendly unicorns?" Mara asks.

"Is she serious?" Justin looks to me for an answer.

"If you do, we won't tell anyone if you let us ride one." Trying to loosen the tension, I play along.

With a smile, Justin says, "I remember you weren't too comfortable when you met Cisco. How about I work with you and let Mara have a private lesson with Jeb?"

"You don't have to do that. I'm sure you're busy."

"Not too busy to spend time with you," he says softly.

Mara's sigh is audible, but not as loud as the snort Jeb makes. Justin casts a dirty look at him and Jeb's eyes widen.

"We'll take Dolly over to the other private ring." Justin reaches for her harness like it's a done deal. Leading her to the gate, he swings it open and guides her out. Without the fence barricade, she's much bigger up close. Her head is higher than mine. "You good, Jeb?"

Mara widens her eyes and shakes her head. When she speaks, her voice is pleading. "Don't leave me."

"You're in good hands. Jeb is the horse whisperer around here. And I'll be right over there." Justin points to a small ring across the yard. "I'll keep an eye on you."

The confidence in his voice soothes the raw edges of my nerves. He takes my hand, leading Dolly on his other side.

"It's nice to see you," he says, giving my hand a squeeze.

"I didn't know we were coming here. Mara made the reservation. Riding was all her idea."

He glances over his shoulder. "She doesn't seem too sure about the horses."

"Terrified." *Me too*, a little voice whispers inside of me.

"And you?" He stops us in front of the gate and releases my hand to open it. "Do you want to learn how to ride or were you just appeasing your friend?"

I haven't mentioned my people pleasing habit, but his words hit close to home. "Let's say it's more of a recent interest."

The smile he gives me is slightly wicked and borders on being a cocky smirk. "Oh, really? When did this new interest start? Maybe at a rodeo?"

I narrow my eyes at him. "Those barrel racers are amazing."

He lets out a short laugh and gestures for me to follow him and Dolly into the ring. "I'll be sure to let them know they have a new fan."

The clank of metal latching against metal reminds me I'm now trapped in here.

He catches my glance at the gate and comments, "Put on your helmet. If Dolly goes berserk, run for the fence and slide through the rungs."

"Seriously?" I step away from the two of them.

"No. Dolly's too old for that sort of nonsense." He pats her neck and moves to her side near her shoulders. "Ready?"

"For what?" My voice cracks.

"To ride?"

I'd rather find his cabin and make out for an hour.

He pats the saddle. "Alley-oop!"

"Excuse me?" I don't move.

He steps into my space. Dolly's neck blocks us from view of the other riding rings. I'm grateful for the sense of privacy when Justin wraps his free hand around my waist and pulls me against him right before he kisses me. This isn't a polite peck. His tongue slides into my mouth and I arch into him in response.

"Mmm," he hums against my mouth. "That seemed to do the trick."

I blink open my eyes. "What?"

"Calmed you down. You were making Dolly and me nervous." He releases me with a grin.

"Trickster." I eye the saddle and stirrups. "How am I supposed to get up there?"

"Easy. Put your foot in the stirrup and then straighten your leg so you can swing your other leg over her back."

I stare at him.

"I'll hold her steady. You can do this."

I follow his instructions and almost fall over upside down.

"Okay, let's try this with a boost." He folds his hands together and holds them near the stirrup. "Foot goes here and grip the saddle horn."

Giving him side-eye, I gently rest my boot in his hands.

"You're going to need to shift your weight into it. And don't you dare say or think you're too heavy to lift. Just don't. Ready?"

With a nod, I shift my weight and in a flash, he's lifting me high enough I can swing my leg over Dolly.

"I did it!" I'm a baller. I'm totally savage.

Until Dolly shifts and I nearly slide off the saddle.

"Hold on to something." Justin steadies me with his hand

on my hip. "You're not ready for bareback."

And my mind immediately goes to riding him bareback. Apparently, all horsey things make me horny. Because I have a dirty mind.

I grip the horn as tight as possible, my knuckles turning white.

"Loosen up." Justin pokes my thigh. "Feet in the stirrups. Drop your heels."

So bossy. I glance down at him and then at the position of my hand wrapped around the phallic saddle horn. Yep, that looks dirty too.

"I'm going to lead you around the ring so you can get used to the feel of her gait. Ready? Keep your heels down and your shoulders back."

With a nod, I give him a weak smile. "Giddy up."

Shaking his head, Justin tries to hide his own grin.

"Don't pretend I'm not adorable."

When he clicks his tongue and moves forward, Dolly follows.

"There's no denying it," he says over his shoulder.

"I'm sorry. I couldn't hear you because I'm all the way up here. On this horse. Can you repeat that please?" I let my body sway in rhythm with Dolly's steps.

Justin laughs and shakes his head. "There's no denying you're adorable."

"Why, thank you for the compliment." I grin down at him.

"Tighten your core and don't let yourself move around so much in the saddle. Pay attention to your posture. Your abs and inner thighs should be engaged. You're probably going to be sore tomorrow."

Are you kidding me? How am I supposed to not make that dirty?

To make things worse, Justin's backside is distracting me. There's something about the way old, faded denim curves around the man's ass as he walks. His broad shoulders tug at the tight fabric of his shirt, revealing the cut of his strong back down to his hips.

"Mara seems to be doing okay." His voice pulls me out of my observations. I lift my head and spot Mara upright on Loretta and moving at about the same pace as us. I give her a wave. She lifts a hand to return the gesture and then immediately grips her saddle again.

"Do I look that nervous?" I ask.

Justin twists to study me. "You could relax a little more, but no, you don't look like you're about to die. You look good up there."

His compliment makes me smile.

"Ready to take the reins?"

My smile fades. "I'm not sure I'm ready for that kind of power and control."

"I think you are." He slows and Dolly stops. "It's easy. Keep your calves and feet away from her side, unless you want her to go faster."

I straighten my legs away from her belly faster than he can finish his words, earning a chuckle from him.

"I'll be right here." He flips the reins over her head and hands them to me. "Left rein, turn left. Right to turn right. Hold them both in your dominant hand."

"Dolly, it's me and you. And I want to let you know that I think that girl Jolene is bad news, too." I pat her strong neck.

Justin's shoulders shake with amusement. "I think you two are going to be great friends. I'll be right over there."

As he guides me, he teaches me how to encourage her to walk and how to steer. In a few minutes, I feel my shoulders relax and I exhale deeply for the first time since getting in the saddle.

"Posture." Justin reminds me from his perch on the top rung of the fence.

I tighten my abs and make sure my shoulders are back and my heels are down.

"Good girl."

His praise resonates inside of me, making me grin.

"Slow her down and change directions."

"How?" I look at my hands and wonder where the brakes are.

"Pull back on the reins. And feel free to say whoa."

I catch his grin as I pass by him. "Stop teasing me."

"I'm not. It works."

Dolly slows to a stop.

"Now turn her."

I manage to get her to go left, circling the ring counter clockwise.

Each time we pass Justin, I meet his eyes and feel the impact of his beautiful smile deep in my chest. When he winks at me, I tighten my thighs.

Dolly responds to the pressure and picks up her pace. As she trots around the circle, I bounce in the saddle, trying to keep my posture.

"What did I do?" Panic creeps into my tone.

"Loosen your legs and pull back on the reins." He remains completely calm while I speed around the ring.

I do as he says. She slows to a walk and then meanders over to Justin.

"I'm impressed."

"Whatever I did was an accident." And completely his fault for being so damn sexy.

"You stayed on the horse and didn't freak out."

"I don't think I'm ready for a moving dismount."

Laughing, he jumps down from the fence and lands on his feet like a cat. "I think you're a natural. A couple more lessons and you'll be ready for a trail ride."

"Are you going to give me private lessons?" I try to purr the words and make them sexy.

Slipping the reins out of my hands, he steadies Dolly. "You think I'm going to let Jeb or one of the other guys spend time with you on my ranch? No way."

"How do I get off this thing?" I'd lean down to kiss him, but I'm afraid of falling.

With a hand on Dolly's nose, he puts the other one on the saddle horn. Right between my legs. "Reverse your mount."

All I hear is reverse cowgirl. Because he's close and being charming with his ridiculously beautiful smile and a dangerous spark in his eyes.

I manage to dismount without face-planting. When both feet are firm on the ground, I raise my arms like a gymnast who just stuck her landing off the vault.

"You get a ten from me." Justin grins and gives me a quick kiss.

I press my lips to his and wrap my arms around his shoulders. "Thank you."

"You nailed that landing. You earned it."

He's cute when he's funny. So I kiss him again. Something bumps my head and I jerk away.

"I think Dolly's jealous." Justin half-laughs, half-speaks. I notice his eyes dart over to the other riding rings like he's worried someone spotted us canoodling. Cowboy law probably prohibits things like kissing, canoodling, and cuddling. Especially in front of other cowboys.

Sure enough her big brown nose is inches from our heads.

"Had enough for today?" He pats her nose, gently shoving her head away from my face.

"Definitely." My legs feel a little wobbly.

"Want to stay for lunch?" In the shadow of his cap's brim, his eyes are almost black. For a brief moment I wonder if I'm on the menu.

"Mara's my ride."

Mara. I kind of forgot about her. I turn to check on her in the other area. She's still on Loretta and has a grin on her face. Apparently I'm not the only one who's having fun.

"She's welcome to stay, too."

"Can we watch the rest of her lesson?" I ask.

"Of course. I'll lead Dolly back to the group paddock after taking off her tack. Head over and I'll meet you back there."

I practically skip over to the other riding ring. Partially from joy and partly because my inner thighs are jelly.

Justin must have legs of steel and stamina for days.

NINETEEN

JUSTIN

THE INVITATION SLIPS past my lips before I really think about the repercussions of inviting Zoe to lunch here on the ranch. Hell, evidently, I've already lost my mind kissing her out in the ring.

We can always leave and eat in town. I'm sure Jeb will tell everyone everything. The gossip will travel quicker than a fire through dry grass.

Better to face the mob and stop any rumors before they can gain traction.

Right, okay. I give myself a pep talk while I hang up Dolly's tack.

No, I'm not hiding in the tack room. After organizing a few bridles and harnesses, I admit I might be avoiding facing Jeb again.

The downside of that is I'm wasting the limited time I have with Zoe this week.

When I return to the riding ring, Mara's lesson's over. She's hugging Zoe and both women are jumping up and down.

Holding Loretta's harness, Jeb leads her toward the barn. As we pass, he gives me a sly smile. "Gotta check with Tammy on who had July."

My brows scrunch together. "Huh?"

"The dating pool?" He slaps my shoulder. "Guess it really is Cowboy Christmas for you. She's totally hot. You know if the perky blonde is single?"

"Just met her."

"The blonde?"

"Both."

"Nice." Now he grips my shoulder and shakes me. "Didn't think you were into sharing, but man, you're my hero."

I place my hand over his and squeeze while pulling it off my arm. "First, none of your damn business. Second, I meant I met them both recently, but I'm only interested in Zoe. Third, I regret telling you that. Fourth, keep this to yourself."

"Okay, okay, cranky bastard." With a chuckle, he continues toward the tack room.

With an exhale, I silently tell him off as I stroll back to Zoe.

"You did it!" She gives Mara a double high five.

After their hands touch, Mara points her index fingers like guns, blows on the tips, before putting one and then the other in her back pockets. Like a super happy, cute gunslinger.

Grinning at Zoe, I join them. "No guns allowed in the dining hall. We had to put a sign up by the door."

"Seriously? There was a big enough issue you had to make a sign?" Zoe asks.

"Allegedly, and way before my time, two of the ranch-hands fell for the same woman. Things got ugly. Guns were pulled."

"Did they shoot each other?" Mara's eyes widen.

"Only one of them fired. Hit the wall. Bullet's still lodged in the wood as a reminder."

Both women stare at me with their mouths open.

"Wow. This is the wild west," Zoe says, in awe. "Gunslingers and cowboys. Oh my."

Mara nudges her shoulder and jerks her head toward the corner of the barn. "Ask him."

"Ask me what?"

Zoe shoots a quick glare at her friend. "Nothing."

"You can ask me anything." And I mean it.

"Can you give me a roping demonstration? I saw the dummy by the barn." Zoe won't meet my eyes and instead points off in the distance.

"Sure. We don't have a ton of time before lunch, but I'm always happy to show off."

I grab a loop of practice rope and head over to the roping dummy.

"Make sure you're out of the way. I don't want to accidentally lasso you." I give Zoe a cocky smile.

"Could you?" she says, her voice soft and flirty. The tone makes my pulse quicken.

"Rope you?" I ask, adjusting the loops in my hand. "Is that what you want? To be tied up?"

"I'm going to go find a bathroom. Or an outhouse," Mara mutters. "You two need privacy and I need to not be here."

Her words barely register as she walks away.

Zoe nods her head. "Not the ankle tying part."

Still coiling and uncoiling the rope, I narrow the distance between us. "What is it about the rope?"

"I don't know," she whispers, close enough I can feel her breath on my cheek.

"Is it the control?"

"Maybe," she says so softly I feel more than hear the words.

"Do you want to try it on me? Or is this something you want me to do to you?"

Her thick, dark lashes frame her wide eyes as she slowly blinks.

Fearing I've gone too far, I lean back, giving her space.

"Will it hurt?" she asks

"Not if I do it right." I lower my voice.

"I want to see how it feels." Her chin lifts slightly as she resolves herself.

I quickly press my lips to hers. "This should be interesting."

To warm up, I toss the rope over the dummy's head a few times.

"Ready?" I ask after I'm sure I can do this without giving her rope burns or hitting her in the face.

Inhaling a deep breath, I step away from her and prepare. "Ready?

"Stop asking and do it." She rolls her shoulders back.

The rope sails through the air and I hold my breath until it clears her shoulders. I gently tug on the end and it tightens, but doesn't constrict to the point of pain.

"You okay?" I'm already moving to free her.

"I'm fine. Thanks for indulging me."

I meet her gaze and she smiles at me.

"Next time I tie you up, I'd rather use something softer. Like a silk scarf or velvet."

Her eyes widen into a surprised expression I see on the horses when something spooks them.

"Something I said?"

"I want there to be a next time," she whispers, and then clears her throat. "Yes, please."

My eyebrows lift in surprise. "I've never done that with a woman."

Images of her golden skin on white sheets, her dark hair splayed on my pillow, and her hands tied with a soft ribbon float through my mind. My body reacts and stirs at the thought of her willingly giving me control.

"What are you doing now?" I ask, my voice suddenly raspy.

The damn triangle clangs, signaling the stampede for lunch.

"Guess we're eating lunch." She frowns as she steps out of the loose rope.

"Or I could throw you over my shoulder and carry you back to my cabin." Silently I chant for her to pick my option.

"Tempting, but I don't want to be the kind of friend who ditches my friend because of a hot cowboy. Today was monumental for Mara. We need to celebrate."

"I respect that." At least mentally. My body is about to stage a revolt. It's a good thing my dick doesn't have a mind of its own or the capability to overrule rational thought.

"Thank you." She kisses my cheek, lingering the pressure of her lips on my skin.

The shadow of the barn provides us some privacy, so I circle my arms around her and pull her closer. Ducking my head near her ear, I inhale the sweet floral and spice scent of her. "You might not thank me after lunch. Prepare yourself."

She gives me a quizzical expression. "Why?"

"Don't worry. It's me who's about to get hooeyed." I slip my fingers between hers and curl our hands together.

"Mind if I wash up first? I'm a little horsey."

"You're perfect just as you are." I give her a quick kiss. "But I agree about the stench. We'll stop at the bathrooms."

Her horrified expression makes me laugh. "I'm kidding about the smell. Come on, we don't want to be late."

"What does hooeyed mean?" Zoe asks as we step onto the porch of the dining hall.

"It's a roping term when three of the calf's legs are tied together. Same thing as a half-hitch, but hooey's more fun to say."

"I agree." She squeezes my fingers as if she senses my nervousness.

I return her grip. Guiding her through the screen door,

I'm careful to not let it slam shut behind us. Less to do with Tammy's wrath and more to avoid drawing attention to us.

Only a few people stand in line for the buffet. A lot of the team is out on day rides or on their way back from the Saturday overnight trips. Less than half the tables are full. We easily spot Mara sitting with Jeb. Zoe gives her friend a wave and I glower at Jeb, silently telling him to mind his manners.

He frowns. I'm not a master at reading lips, but it looks like he mouths *"boyfriend"* to me. Poor Jeb. Shot down once again.

As the line moves forward, I keep an eye on the swinging door to the kitchen. The sound of conversation and silverware scraping on plates fills the room. No one stares at me or Zoe. There's no whispering or pointing. Everything seems normal.

Then the door opens and Tammy pushes through with a fresh tray of rolls.

When she sees me, her eyes immediately focus on where my hand is wrapped around Zoe's.

"Sweet corn and honey!" she shouts and promptly drops the tray on the floor. "Well, fuck."

Bread bounces and rolls across the worn wood planks. "Language, Tammy."

"I tried!" She sets down the tray. "You can't scare an old woman like this. I could have palpitations."

I laugh as she dramatically clutches her chest.

"Don't you mock your elders," she scolds. "Now introduce me to your friend."

"Zoe, this is Tammy. Tammy, this is Zoe. She and her friend Mara just finished their first riding lesson."

"Good for you!" Tammy hugs Zoe, pulling her away from my grip as she turns her to get a better look. "Aren't you a pretty one. Where'd he find you?"

Zoe glances at me nervously.

"I picked her up hitchhiking."

"Oh, that's dangerous. Please tell me he's joking. Buzz has a weird sense of humor and I can never tell if he's serious."

"It's partially true. Our ride ditched us and Justin showed up like a knight in shining armor to rescue us."

Tammy looks me over. "He did? Isn't that nice of him?"

"I can be nice," I protest.

"Can and do are two different things." Tammy steers Zoe toward the food. "We're out of rolls, but you should try my green enchiladas with chicken. Unless you're a vegetarian, then we have salad and some beans. I swear I don't put lard in them. Or I can make you a cheese quesadilla. Do you eat dairy?"

Never in my life have I heard Tammy be so accommodating about food. She'll make vegetarian and gluten free options for the catering side of things, but her typical policy is if you don't like it, don't eat it. At least until she decides she likes someone.

There's no way she's already to the point of liking Zoe. Not after meeting her forty seconds ago.

Zoe takes a plate and puts a little of everything on it. Either she's hungry or being polite.

I heap three enchiladas, rice and beans on my own plate, then pour more green sauce over the top.

"What do you want to drink, hon?" Tammy asks.

"Arnold Palmer, like usual," I answer her.

She's focused on Zoe and her tone is exasperated when she speaks. "Not you. You drink the same thing every day. Why would I bother asking?"

"I'll have the same," Zoe says. "Point me in the right direction and I'll get it for us."

"You go sit. I'll bring it over." Tammy shoos her away.

I remain standing near the buffet with my mouth open.

"You catching flies?" Tammy brushes past me.

"Who are you?" I ask her.

"Hush. I'm being welcoming to your friend." She winks

and gives me a knowing smile. "Or should I say girlfriend?"

My eyes dart to Zoe, hoping she's out of earshot of Tammy's teasing. "We just met."

"Does it matter? When was the last time you held hands with a woman in this dining hall?"

"College? That summer I dated the Italian exchange student?"

"Wrong. Never." She moves to pinch my cheek, something she hasn't done since I was a kid. "I'm so happy I could burst."

I squint at her. "What date did you have in the pool?"

"Never you mind."

"How much money will you stand to make?" I call after her as she ignores me and hurries back into the kitchen.

She can run, but she can't hide. A smile tugs at my mouth as I weave my way through the tables to where Zoe and Mara sit.

"You survive?" Zoe asks when I sit next to her.

"Barely. You?"

"Tammy seems nice. Motherly."

Jeb chokes on his water. "If your mother is a mountain lion. Don't mess with her."

"She's not that—" I cut myself off. "No, she is that bad. But if she loves you, she does it fiercely."

"Zoe's the same way." Mara grins at her friend.

TWENTY

ZOE

I OWE MARA a thank you cake or some gratitude cupcakes after she happily agreed Justin should bring me home.

Because the man not only drove me, but is giving me one hell of a good-bye kiss in front of the condo.

We're basically making out in the middle of the day on a charming side street with tourists and snobby residents passing by. Pretty sure public sex is frowned upon by the hoity and the toity around here.

Justin creates a breath of distance between our mouths. "I don't want your neighbors to call the cops on me."

"Oh, don't worry about it. I don't even live here." As the last word leaves my mouth, I mentally try to pull it back in like it's tethered to me by a string.

"What the hell?" He leans away from me. Or as far as he can get with my hands in his back pockets.

I release my grip, and he creates polite distance between our bodies while waiting for me to explain.

"I'm dog and house sitting. The condo belongs to my best friend, Sage, who's gone for a month. I could never afford a condo in Aspen. On my own." I let it all spill out.

With his arms crossed, he leans against the wall. "You said you had a roommate."

"I did. In my last place. Only he was also my boyfriend."

"The jerk?"

I nod.

"How long ago?"

"At the end of the ski season. He went back to Chicago at the beginning of May. I stayed until our lease was up in July. When Sage and Lee come home, I'll be homeless."

"No, you won't. You can have a cabin on the ranch. I think we have an empty one or two. If not, I'll make a couple of the guys bunk together."

"You can't do that." I'm stunned he'd offer me a place.

"It's my family's ranch, so I can. You're not going to be without a place to live."

"I've been looking for a roommate situation down valley."

"How's that going?" His mouth turns down.

"I think a lot of them are creepy men who want a maid who they can also have sex with. Or girlfriends who split the rent."

"You'd rather pay rent to a weirdo than take one of my cabins?" He twists his mouth and nods. "I'm not sure whether or not I should be insulted or impressed with your stubborn independence."

"Don't be insulted. Can we continue this conversation while I walk the dogs?"

He nods, but doesn't move.

"I'll be right back."

Inside, I dash down the hall to the bathroom and splash water on my face as I wash my hands. I give myself a sniff—I'm definitely horsey—and decide to apply more deodorant. My cheeks are flushed in my reflection and my once neat braid is loose and messy. I'm thoroughly a mess.

Untying my hair, I switch to a messy bun and accept this

is how I've looked the entire time I've been with Justin today. No point in trying to fix myself up now.

I release the hounds from their crates and leash them up. For a minute, I imagine Justin leaving the second I dashed inside. A guy like him who loves the simple life doesn't need all my baggage. I'm sure the homelessness and housesitting fibs are the final straw.

But there he is, standing in the same spot I left him, staring out at the street, completely at ease.

"You stayed."

Excited to see him again, Hunter and Nell try to jump on his legs. I feel the same way.

He didn't run away.

"Where else would I be?" He gives me a sweet smile. "You can't chase me away that easily. Don't you remember our conversation at dinner the other night? Complicated is my family's motto. Do I wish you didn't lie to me? Absolutely. But I understand not wanting to dump out your personal luggage to a stranger."

"I promise I'm not keeping any other skeletons from you."

He nods. "Good."

He might be a keeper after all.

Justin's kisses are my new favorite thing. Unfortunately, he's out of town again. I'm left with the memory of his last goodbye kiss and a phone full of text messages. I'm going to need new batteries soon. I mentally add them to my shopping list.

Good news is it's Wednesday and that means he's back for the Snowmass rodeo. Mae and Mara have agreed to come with me. For the record, there was zero arm twisting involved to get them to agree.

After working all morning, I'm driving down valley to do

some grocery shopping and pick up more dog treats. Either those dogs are manipulating me for cookies, or Sage didn't leave enough supplies.

My phone rings and I glance at the screen. The number is unfamiliar but local. I hit the screen on the dash and answer.

"Is this Zoe Saragossa?" a woman's voice asks after I answer.

"Yes?" I echo her tone.

"This is Emily Mays. From Ashcroft Ranch."

I'm on a winding stretch of 82 where I can't pull over, but I really, really need to focus on this call. Ahead I spot a bus stop and pull into it so I can concentrate.

"Hi." My voice cracks.

"I'm so happy I caught you. We're thrilled to be able to offer you a residency at Ashcroft for the late summer session."

"For next year?" My heart races at the prospect of spending part of next summer there.

"It's extremely short notice, but we have an opening for this year. Starting in a week. Are you available the beginning of August? The board was unanimous when we reviewed your portfolio. That rarely happens."

The rush of blood in my ears makes it almost impossible for me to hear and process her words.

"Hello? Are you there? Hello? Did we lose the connection?" Her voice sounds far away.

"I'm here." The words come out all breathy.

"If you have time, maybe we could meet in person and I can give you a tour. I'm available this afternoon. I realize you may be unavailable, but please consider joining us." It almost sounds like she's begging.

"I can come by the ranch in an hour."

"Perfect!" Her voice becomes chipper. "Wonderful. I'm in the main office. I'll see you when you get here."

We say our good-byes, and I pinch my thigh to keep from

screaming until I hang up.

Then I let out the loudest howl of happiness ever.

I even dance in my seat, pumping my arms in the open air of the sunroof.

The loud horn of the bus honking behind me douses my solo car party with a bucket of harsh reality. Waving, I ease away from the bus stop and back into traffic. Groceries and dog treats will have to wait. I need to get home and change out of my cut-offs and halter top. Because I'm going to Ashcroft.

I scream again and blare the radio.

Miley Cyrus and I are singing a kickass duet of "Party in the USA" as I drive back into Aspen. I crank up the volume, blasting music with my windows down. When Miley tells me to put my hands up, I do. Because we're a couple of girls living our dreams.

This girl right here is going to be an artist in residence at Ashcroft Ranch for the whole month of August.

An entire month to create and live in the studio again. The timing couldn't be more perfect. August is the start of the slow down before off season. My manager won't give me a hard time about being gone, and the other therapists will be happy to not fight for hours. If my regulars need an appointment, I can make time.

When Miley breaks into the chorus, I let loose . . . not caring I'm stuck in traffic and people are probably staring.

I'm tempted to stand up and yell my good news, but somehow I doubt anyone will be as excited as I am.

The cars to the left of mine move ahead and I have lane choice regret. I check my mirrors and glance to my left to see if I can slide over. Putting on my blinker, I slide closer to the middle. The big gray truck flashes their lights to let me know I can cut over. I wave out the sunroof. They honk and I pull forward. Once I have enough space between us, I check out the kind stranger through my rearview mirror.

Leaning his forearms on the steering wheel, Justin grins back at me.

I have to hit the brakes hard to avoid hitting the car in front of mine. Feeling sheepish, I meet Justin's eyes again in the mirror. So close and we're trapped in our vehicles. It's been a whole three days since we've seen each other. Seventy-two hours feels like a month.

As we creep forward, my phone rings. His name appears on the screen. I hit accept and meet his eyes again.

"So you're a big Miley Cyrus fan?" His deep voice fills my car.

"You saw that?" My cheeks heat and I wonder if he can see.

"Saw and heard. I even have video of it on my phone."

"Noo!" I screech. "Delete!"

"It's adorable. When I'm missing you, I can watch it."

"And remember I'm a goofball?"

"What made you so happy? Or are you Miley's number one fan?"

I grin. "I want to tell you in person."

"Can you give me a hint?"

The low timbre of his voice makes it difficult to resist him.

"No." I tease and watch as he pouts out his full bottom lip.

"Fine. Come up to the ranch and tell me there. I need to get ready for the rodeo."

"I want to, I really do, but I can't. I have to be in Snowmass in less than an hour."

"Is that a hint?"

"Maybe."

"This seems entirely unfair to see you and not be able to kiss you." He groans. "Now I'm going to have to get through an entire competition tonight before we can spend time together?"

There's a slight edge of frustration or maybe even desperation to his voice. Ahead, traffic has completely stopped.

I shove the car into park and undo my seatbelt. With full knowledge I'm about to create a bigger traffic mess, I jump out and run over to his truck.

Shock and then understanding covers Justin's face when he sees what I'm doing. He leans out the truck's window at the same time I climb on the running board and press my lips to his.

Our kiss is brief, but worth it. Horns behind and next to us start honking as I jog back to my car.

"That was one helluva kiss." His voice carries through the speakers.

I meet his eyes again in the rearview mirror. "I agree."

Finally, traffic eases up as we enter the rotary.

"I'll try to find you before the events begin." Smiling, I keep eye contact until his truck takes the first right and heads toward the Highlands.

"Promise? It's stupid because it's only been a couple of days, but I've missed you. Texting sucks."

Even though he can't see me anymore, I grin at his words. "I agree."

"Just a few more hours until I . . ." His voice breaks up and I can't hear the rest of what he says. The call disconnects a few seconds later.

Once I get home, I text a sad face about getting disconnected. He responds with "soon."

One word from him can make me swoon.

I'm in deep and we've only kissed.

TWENTY-ONE

JUSTIN

LIFE IN A small town's funny. Zoe and I have lived here for the past couple of years, but haven't run into each other. Or maybe we have and didn't notice before. Now that we've met and spent some time together, we see each other all over the place, including stuck in traffic. Makes me wonder how many other times we've been in the same place, but didn't pay attention.

It amazes me how we can live parallel lives in the same place. I wonder what else I'm missing out on by sequestering myself up at the ranch.

With a grin permanently slapped on my face from Zoe's unexpected kiss, I follow the road while it twists and turns heading to the Easy Z.

My phone rings and without checking the screen, I assume it's Zoe reconnecting our dropped call.

"Hello, beautiful. Miss me?" I chuckle at how sappy I sound.

"I always miss you," my grandmother responds. "Thank you for calling me beautiful. A woman never gets tired of hearing it."

I swear I'm probably blushing. "It's nice to hear your voice. How's Santa Fe?"

"It's a dry heat." Her laugh sounds like antique bells. "The international crafts show is this week, so I'm in the middle of the hullabaloo bullshit."

"You love it. I'm sure you're invited to every party."

She sighs, but I hear the smile in her voice. "It's exhausting. I'm looking forward to escaping in a few weeks."

"Coming to see your favorite grandson, I hope."

"The one who's never home and always risking his life on the back of an angry male beast? I'm sure a psychiatrist could write a book about father issues in rodeo cowboys."

"I think I'll be out of town during your visit," I grumble.

"What happened to missing me?" she teases.

"Tammy spilled the beans about the betting pool. Are you hoping to collect your winnings while you're here?" Might as well call her on her role when I don't have to meet her eyes.

She laughs again. "That woman can't keep a secret."

"True, but she knows most of ours, so we better keep her around."

"Or bury the body where no one will find it," she says dryly.

Ah, there's the famous Garrison humor.

"You can't say things like that in polite company."

"You're not company, and even though I raised you right, you're not always polite. I've been hearing grumblings of your foul mood all the way down here."

"No one's quit." I pull the truck into my spot near the cabin.

"Yet. I could quote you some bull dookie about honey and flies, but you already know these things."

"Yes, Grandmother."

Her annoyance echoes in the silence.

"Fine, I'll work on it."

"You're a Garrison. Charm runs in your veins along with the famous anger. Use it."

I hate when she reminds me of the dark side of my legacy. "Yes, ma'am."

"Good. Now tell me about this young lady you kissed at the ranch." Her voice softens. "Tammy says she's lovely. City girl?"

"I think I'm losing you. Bad connection." I chuckle.

"Nice try, but I'm not falling for that trick again. I'm looking forward to meeting her in a few weeks when I'm in town for the Ashcroft board meeting."

"It's on my calendar."

"Wonderful. I need to go. The Carltons will be here soon. We're having cocktails before the gala tonight and I need to decide which caftan won't make me look like an old woman."

"You'll be the prettiest belle at the ball."

"There's the charm. Save it for your lady. I love you."

"Love you," I say before we end the call.

My grandmother is one of a kind and I don't know what I'd do without her.

It takes a moment for me to realize I've agreed to introduce her to Zoe in a couple of weeks.

TWENTY-TWO

ZOE

MY MEETING WITH Emily goes well and when I leave, I'm officially an Ashcroft artist in residence.

Sage is my first call. I wait for her to appear on FaceTime.

A very rumpled blond head of hair appears on the dark screen. "Zoe? Are the dogs okay?"

"Shit. I didn't even think of the time." I check the clock in the car. "Oh crap. It's like one in the morning. They're fine."

With a yawn, Sage waves at me before the video cuts to a pillow and a dark head of hair.

"Hold on," she whispers close to the screen so all I see is her chin and teeth.

She freezes on the screen for a second but I think I can still hear muffled sounds. I whisper back. "Hello?"

A light turns on behind Sage and the soft sound of a door clicking shut echoes through the phone.

"Hi." She waves again.

"Are you in a closet?"

"Bathroom. Are you sure the dogs are okay?"

"Fine. Maybe a little fatter. I think I'm being played for treats."

She smiles like a proud mom whose child won the spelling bee. "They're very smart. Hold on, I'm going to mute you while I pee. I figure I might as well go while I'm up. Tell me why you're calling. I miss your face."

More shifting of the camera and I stare up at the bathroom ceiling for a few seconds before she returns.

"I got into Ashcroft." I try to make my voice sound normal and not like I've been inhaling helium. "For next month."

My view swings through the air and now I'm on the floor, staring at Sage's knee. Her head appears. She's saying something, maybe even screaming, and her eyes are bugged out.

After a minute of her flailing, grinning, and maybe screaming, she frowns. Shifting around, she says something more to whatever's on her left. I mime she's still on mute.

Laughing, she turns her mic on. "Sorry about that. Lee says congrats, since he's apparently the only one who heard me yelling with joy."

"I've missed you so much. You're never allowed to leave me for this long. Two weeks. Tops."

"Agree." She grins. "But it sounds like you're doing awesome without me. I'm so excited for you. Can I come hang out in your studio and stare at you? Ooh, even better, can we recreate the pottery wheel scene from *Ghost*?"

"We both hate that movie and Patrick Swayze's ugly maroon shirt for eternity." I smile back at her.

"Speaking of men, what's going on with the cowboy?"

I've kept her updated with emails and texts, but nothing since the ranch.

"We made out in front of horses at his ranch."

"Sounds serious?" she asks.

"Maybe? I don't know. I'm seeing him at the rodeo tonight."

"Is that why you're all prettified?"

"I had my interview at Ashcroft." I brush imaginary lint off of my dusty rose summer dress.

"You're beautiful. And he looks dreamy from the Google stalking."

I love how she openly admits this like it's not at all creepy.

"Hopefully he'll still be around when you get home. When is that? Some time next year?"

"Nice sarcasm." She rolls her eyes. "Next week. When do you start at the ranch?"

"Soon. I'll be moving into my little cabin right after you get back."

"You can always crash in our guest room."

"You're the best. Except when you leave me to go to the other side of the world. How is it?"

"Beautiful, different, kind of the same. Except we saw lions and elephants when we went on safari. Everyone sounds like Lee." Her smile is completely content. "But I miss home. Hunter. Nell. You. The mountains."

When she yawns again, I feel bad for keeping her up. "Go back to sleep. We'll talk soon. Love you. Hi to Lee."

"Love you." She covers her yawn with the back of her hand before giving me one more sleepy wave.

Still wanting to share my good news, I call my parents. Mom answers on the home phone.

"Mom, Momma!"

"Zoe?" She says my name without the *e* at the end. "What's going on? Are you okay? Do you need money?"

My excitement deflates like a popped balloon. "I'm fine and thanks, but I have a job."

"I know, but how much money can you be making? We worry."

I'm regretting phoning her and we're ten seconds into the call. "I have good news."

"Oh, honey. Are you finally moving home? We've been

hoping now that Neil is back in Chicago you'll come to your senses and come home. You know, your dad ran into him at the club. He asked about you. I think you could work things out if you stop being stubborn and just talk to him."

Ignoring her jabs, I share my good news in hopes it will change her mind. "I got the Ashcroft residency. A month at the ranch, with a stipend and a little cabin of my own. Plus, I'm guaranteed to be part of the annual show in Denver this fall. At the art museum. Isn't that amazing?"

"That's wonderful. So you'll move home after? I don't think the high altitude is good for you long term. There are studies showing negative effects. Your brain needs more oxygen."

"The Nepalese Sherpas seem to be fine."

"Hmm. Who was talking about Nepal? Every year people die on Everest. Kind of proves my point, doesn't it?" I can picture her self-satisfied smirk.

I don't waste any more energy on trying to get through to her. "Thanks, Mom. Share the good news with Dad."

"Okay. I will. When are you coming home to visit?"

Never, I think.

"Probably not until the off season in the fall."

"It would be nice to have you home for Christmas. Every year you make up an excuse."

I can't get off the phone quick enough. "I'm late to meet the girls at the rodeo. Sorry, I have to go. Love you, Mom. Love to Dad!"

Without waiting for her to reciprocate or not, I end the call.

That went well. Flipping off my phone doesn't help.

I guess when I was a kid, the arts were fine, but as a grown-up, I'm supposed to fall in line. I never realized before how much Neil sounds like my parents. Or they sound like him. Maybe they can adopt him.

I'm not going to let her sour my mood. I repeat this as I drive down the hill to the rodeo grounds.

I'm not going to let her sour my mood.

It doesn't help. A thousand miles away and Mom has the power to ruin my day. It's her superpower.

When I arrive at Town Park, the parking lot is only half full as people begin to trickle in for the evening's festivities. Some come for the barbecue dinner and bar, while families entertain their kids on the mini bull ride and kids' activities.

Grumpy and annoyed, I head straight for the bar and order a lemonade with yummy Marble Gingercello. Like limoncello but with ginger, the drink packs a punch even mellowed with the sweet lemonade. I finish half of it while I standing at the bar. My phone chirps with a text as I consider getting another one to save time.

The girls are on their way, but still at Mara's.

Pointing to my cup, I gesture to the bartender for another drink. I leave a tip for both and mosey in the direction of the horse trailers. The booze hits my bloodstream and I remember I haven't eaten since breakfast.

Whee. I'm a cheap drunk tonight. Feeling better and re-solved to have fun tonight, I weave through the trucks and trailers until I get to the Easy Z area. An older guy with a walrus mustache blocks my path.

"Are you lost? The ladies' port-a-potties are back there." He points behind me.

"You're the walrus." I grin at him. "I'm Zoe."

He doesn't return my greeting or smile. "Nice to meet you. If you're wanting a new buckle for your collection, you're going to have to wait until after the show, sweetheart."

Sweetheart? Buckle? "Oh, I'm not a buckle bunny. And I'm not sure if I should take that as a compliment or not." I glance down to make sure my boobs aren't hanging out and my top didn't become cropped without my knowledge. "I'm here to see Justin."

"There you are," the man himself says, stepping around the mustachioed gatekeeper I assume is his mentor. "Gentry, this is Zoe."

Justin kisses my cheek. "What's in the cup?"

"Ginger lemonade. Want some?" I offer it to him.

"Thanks, but no drinking before competition," Gentry chastises me before walking away. What I really don't need right now is authority figures telling me what to do and judging me.

"More for me." I lift my glass in a mocking toast.

Justin studies me out of the corner of his eye. "Everything okay?"

"Best day ever." I take a sip of my adult beverage. Because I'm an adult.

"What's your good news?" he asks, excitement clear in his voice.

"I got a fellowship at Ashcroft!"

"That's amazing." Justin scoops me up in his arms, leans me back, and plants a smackeroo of a kiss on my lips. I barely have enough brain cells to cling to his shoulder with my free hand before I swoon and spill most of my drink on the ground. "I'm so proud of you."

When he stands me back on my own feet, he doesn't let go. Which is smart because I'm definitely feeling the influence of his kiss and the Gingercello.

"For next summer?" he asks.

"More like next month. I start the first of August." I grin. "How?"

"The director called me today and said they had a cancellation. Because I'm already local, they pushed me to the top of the waitlist."

His arms tighten around my waist. "We need to celebrate."

"I'm always up for cake."

"I'm thinking more of a weekend together."

"With cake?" I can't let it go. I'm tipsy and more than a little hungry. Not quite hangry, but edging toward cranky. Crangy.

He gives me a soft peck. "We can have cake."

"Go on." I kiss him on one corner of his mouth and then the other.

"You, me, horses, and the back country. Alone. Without interruptions." He nuzzles my jaw and softly kisses the skin behind my ear.

I shiver.

His warm breath tickles my ear when he whispers, "Doesn't that sound like heaven?"

Heaven?

No, it sounds like hell.

Except for the part about being alone with him for an entire weekend. We could do that in a hotel. With room service and fresh towels delivered with a simple phone call.

You can take a city girl to the mountains, but it doesn't mean you can make her camp. Or like it.

How far am I willing to go outside my comfort zone for this hot cowboy?

"It sounds—"

"Zoe!" a familiar angry male voice shouts from a few feet away.

There's no fucking way.

"Shit." I jerk away from Justin like I've been shocked.

When he steps back, his eyes blaze at me, and I know my expression matches the sudden guilt that is spreading through my body.

"Who's that?" Justin stares over my shoulder.

"I don't know?" My voice rises at the end, forming a lie. I know that voice and it belongs to the last man I expect to see at a rodeo.

TWENTY-THREE

ZOE

"YOU'RE ASKING ME?" Justin asks, removing his hat and brushing a hand over his head. "Seems like he knows you from the way he's glaring at me."

"Zoe! I've been looking all over for you." Neil's panting like he's been running when he stops next to me. "You're a hard woman to surprise."

I hope he chokes on the lack of air. Thankfully he doesn't touch me. I barely glance at him, keeping my focus on Justin. Unfortunately, Justin's glaring at Neil, completing the uncomfortable triangle.

Being polite, Justin sticks out his hand. "Justin Garrison."

Neil pauses and then doesn't reciprocate. "Nice to meet you. If you don't mind, I'm going to pass on the handshake."

Instead, he offers his fist for Justin to bump. Like he's cool or down with the kids. He's neither.

The edges of my vision darken. I've zoomed past seeing red to blacking out from rage.

"He's afraid of getting his hands dirty," I explain through clenched teeth.

Justin misses my eye roll, but Neil catches it.

"Can't be too careful." Neil bumps his elbow against my arm.

"Don't touch me," I snap, my voice almost a silent growl.

"Right. You do you." Justin finally meets my eyes. "You okay?"

I want to beg him not to leave me with Neil. Just because he's shown up here doesn't mean I have to deal with him, right?

Justin dips his head to study my face. "I've got to get ready. Need to focus."

He surprises me by leaning down and planting a kiss on my lips, then bending me back with his hand between my shoulders.

My head spins again when he sets me upright. I'm not sure if it's from my body's reaction to his kiss or my mind trying to process the declaration. Talk about marking territory.

I'm no longer a bull fantasizing about goring Neil with my horns. But now my hormones are at war with logic. I should be annoyed Justin did that. I'm sure part of me is. Mostly I want to kiss him again and forget Neil's standing here.

Returning his hat to his head, Justin dips the brim at me. "I'll talk to you soon, Zoe."

Talk. Not see.

His tone is ice and he doesn't bother to acknowledge Neil, who seethes next to me, his hands balled into fists. I bet he's never thrown a punch in his life.

I attempt to drain the rest of my spiked lemonade and find the cup empty.

"What are you doing here?" I finally address Neil. "Wait. Don't answer that. I need another drink first."

Without waiting for him, I head toward the bar tent.

"I'm here to see you. Obviously." He catches up and tries to hold my hand. *Are you fucking kidding me?* "I think I explained that when you were making puppy eyes at the cowboy."

"I don't make dog eyes. At anyone." I twist and weave my way to the end of the makeshift bar. I could leave. Walk right out of here and drive away. But I've been drinking and standing around the shuttle stop might be the lamest dramatic getaway ever.

Fine. Another drink it is. The girls will be here soon. Reinforcements to keep me from shoving Neil into a pen with an actual angry bull.

My bartender from earlier spots me. Holding up my empty cup, I gesture for another. He grins and nods.

"Get me one, too," Neil says from my side.

I wonder if I can inflict serious damage with a cocktail sword.

"Please," I snarl at him as I motion to make it two drinks.

"What is it?" he asks when I hand him a cup. His nose wrinkles when he sniffs it. "I know I'm not going to like this. Can I get a beer?"

His voice is loud in my ear when he shouts at the bartender. He's being rude and it's embarrassing. Digging into my purse, I pull out money for the drinks and extra for a nice tip for letting us cut the line. I take the second cup and decide it's a sign I need to double-fist to get through this encounter.

Neil doesn't move to pay.

"It's too crowded in here." I turn to go, not caring if he follows or disappears.

"Hold up! I came here to see you, why do you keep walking away from me?"

I speed up. "I need to meet the girls. We had plans."

"I know," he says. "Your mom told me."

I finally understand the meaning of apoplectic.

When I stop abruptly, he knocks my arm, spilling most of one of my drinks, which further pisses me off. My voice rises into a screech. "She did what?"

"I flew in earlier this afternoon and took a cab to the spa. You weren't there."

"I had the afternoon off." *And it's none of your business.*

"Where are you living? Your mom said with Sage, but isn't she with Lee? I thought they had big plans to go to Cape Town."

My steps falter. Too many questions and assumptions are coming out of Neil like we're catching up after not seeing each other for a couple of weeks. Not him showing up because *my mother* ratted me out. "What are you doing here? I mean in Snowmass, not literally here at the rodeo. Shouldn't you be at work in Chicago?"

"Didn't your mom tell you I ran into your dad at the country club? We had a great talk, and he gave me some strong advice."

"I hope some of his words were about getting your head out of your ass." I finish the remainder of the half-spilled drink and stack the two cups.

"Yeah, that was part of it. But he mostly told me what a mistake I made leaving you out here. How disappointed they are in me."

I pause to gape at him. "Too late, but I'll have to tell him thanks."

"And then he told me to be a man, come to Aspen, and bring you home."

Mentally, I cancel the thank you to my father.

As I process the statement, I start chuckling. Soon, I'm full out, bent over, wheezing while laughing. When I stand back up, Neil, in his Brooks Brothers' shirt and khakis, is glancing around to see who's watching the crazy woman lose her mind.

"You're making a scene," he chastises me through clenched teeth. "Are you drunk?"

"Oh, boy. You're funny." Trying to inhale, I snort, which sends me into another fit of laughing. By the time I can even think about speaking, I'm wiping tears and mascara from under my eyes.

"People are staring," he barks under his breath. "What's wrong with you? Are you willing to throw away five years?"

"Me?" My voice cracks. "You can't seriously think you could fly in here to tell me my dad told you to bring me home, and I'd say okay. I'm not a child. I'm a twenty-six-year-old woman. You called quits. You left. There's nothing but scorched earth left of our relationship."

A few people jostle past us, bumping into his shoulder or mine. Kids wearing mini chaps and hats race through the crowd. We're surrounded by happy people because the rodeo is a happy, magical place. And Neil is ruining it for me.

He grips my arm, not to the point of bruising, but tighter than expected. "I've only been gone for three months, and you're flirting with anything with a dick? How hard up are you? A random bartender and a cowboy? Did you see that guy's dirty hands? There's probably cow shit under his nails. Disgusting."

"We don't even own cattle on the ranch." Justin grabs Neil's hand and pulls his fingers back. "But I know bullshit when I see it. Now take your hand off the lady."

TWENTY-FOUR

JUSTIN

I MADE SURE to catch Neil's eye before they left, letting him know he's on my territory here. My stomach churns watching Zoe walk away with the tool in the office casual clothes trailing after her. I haven't been in a fight in years, but I want to clock that arrogant asshole.

I'm about to follow her when Gentry steps in my path and lectures me about focus. The entire time he speaks about focus, my mind processes what the hell just happened. Takes me five minutes of nodding and giving him half-hearted "yes sirs" before I can escape.

I know Zoe broke up with the boyfriend after ski season, but she's never given any indication she's heartbroken and pining for the ex.

Unless I've missed all the signals.

Sure, we're taking things slow, but that's been mutual. Nothing in my life is rushed, and I certainly don't believe in hurrying love.

Sometimes falling in love is slow like a late summer stream. Other times it roars a path of destruction as it crashes and speeds through life. I prefer the first kind. Still wild and free, this love creates a sense of peace and belonging. A sense of home for my soul.

I kissed her in front of him to prove I could.

A kiss doesn't mean she's mine. Not if her heart belongs to another man.

I fight the urge to run through the crowd and chase her down.

She's not my girlfriend.

We haven't gotten that far yet.

Doesn't matter. I keep an eye on the corner of the rodeo grounds where I saw Zoe disappear into the bar tent. Even as Gentry continues to talk at me while I do my pre-competition check, my focus returns to the tent. Maybe her girlfriends are in there already. I have zero doubts Mae has Zoe's back. Same for Mara.

I'm squatting down by Cisco—checking his hooves and tack—when loud, hysterical laughter echoes from the public areas.

On the surface, it's laughter, but beneath there's an edge of discomfort. Like the sound an animal makes when it's under attack or in pain.

I stand up so quickly, I spook Cisco a little. Alert, his ears swivel back and forth while his eyes dart from me to the crowd. Patting his neck, I calm him. "I'm going to go check it out."

I follow the laughter through the crowd until I spot Zoe. She's wiping tears from her eyes. Neil's grip is tight enough his fingers are making indents on her arm.

Unacceptable.

As I jog over to them, I hear him accuse her of slutting around after their break up. If he broke up with her, then it's none of his damn business.

When he insults me, I almost laugh.

"We don't even have cattle on the ranch." I lower my voice

while I peel his hand off her arm. "But I know bullshit when I see it. Now take your hand off the lady."

Zoe laughs. Her normal, beautiful laugh.

Neil stares at my hand gripping his with disgust.

"Oops, guess I should've washed up." I point over by the toilet trailers. "I'm sure you can find some hand sanitizer around here somewhere."

I don't even acknowledge his slut shaming comment. If I do, I'll probably punch him. The trouble isn't worth it.

"You okay?" I focus on Zoe. Her mascara is smudged and her cheeks are flushed. Could be from the alcohol or Neil. Maybe both.

Honestly, it's none of my business.

I sure as hell want her to be mine, but this breaks my no complications rule.

She nods and steps to my side. "Neil showed up unexpectedly tonight."

"I'd like some privacy so Zoe and I can continue our conversation. If you don't mind." Neil glowers at me.

"Sadly, I do. If it's all right with her, I'd prefer to stay. Her call."

Neil's head jerks back, and then his chin points up like a defiant toddler. Or horse.

Unlike an angry horse, I don't think he's going to charge me. Doesn't mean I'm not prepared to take a hit. My guess is this khaki wearing asshole fights dirty. I remember his type from business school. The Neils of the world are one of the biggest reasons I refuse to work for anyone but family.

"I'm okay." Zoe squeezes my hand. "I swear."

The speakers crackle and squawk as tonight's announcers begin their introductions.

"Looks like it's showtime." I'm reluctant to leave her with Neil. "Mara and Mae showing up tonight? I'll look for you in the stands."

I say the words as a reminder she won't be alone for long with her ex.

"They should be here soon." She steps close and gives me a quick kiss on the cheek. Softly, for only me to hear, she whispers, "Thank you. I'm fine."

Reluctantly, I head back to the trailer. On the way I pass Jim, the rodeo clown, and stop him. "See the brunette over there? The beautiful one in the gingham shirt and jeans? Can you keep an eye on her for me?"

"She's hot. Claiming her early?" He slugs my shoulder.

"We've known each other for a while. The guy with her might start trouble and I want someone to make sure he keeps in line. Or leaves."

"Want me to make him leave? A lot of people get freaked out by clowns. I could stare at him. That might work." Jim grins at me and it's creepy as fuck.

"I appreciate it." With a friendly slap to his back, I continue over to Cisco. Hopefully Gentry hasn't noticed my absence.

I ride like shit tonight.

On the bronco, I barely last my eight seconds. An overcooked spaghetti noodle would have better form than I did.

Before I know it, I'm off the bull and running for the fence.

The only thing that goes my way is roping. Even that I almost mess up because when we enter the arena, I'm scanning the crowd for Zoe instead of focused on the calf. After tying off the final knot, I hold up my arm, still unable to spot her.

"Giving the rest of the guys a shot at a buckle tonight? Feeling generous?" Gentry scowls at me from his spot by the fence.

"Not in the mood for this." I shove past him and the cowboys loitering around.

Jim jogs over to me, his makeup smeared and more hideous. "Your woman left right after you asked me to keep an eye on her."

"With the guy she was with earlier?" Unsettled anxiety fills my lungs with a bad feeling.

"Him, a couple other women and a guy with a beard."

At least it sounds like her friends showed up. I hope they were escorting him to the airport to catch the last flight to Denver tonight.

Knowing I've blown my winning streak, I stomp over to my truck and dig my phone out of the center console.

No messages or missed calls.

My need to know Zoe's okay overrules my need to stay out of any drama. I text her, asking if she's okay.

Gentry knocks on my window. "You came in second. Time to be gracious."

"Always am."

Despite Jim telling me she left, I let my gaze wander while we line up for the final time of the night. Distracted, I manage to clap when Dusty claims his winning buckle. He rode well and earned it.

Once we're off our horses, I congratulate him. "'Bout damn time you got that thing. I was losing faith you'd ever learn how to stay on a bull for longer than one-Mississippi." I might be proud of the kid, but I'm still going to give him shit.

Dusty flashes his teeth in a huge grin. "Won't be the last time."

"We'll see about that." I hold out my hand and he shakes it enthusiastically.

"You gonna join me for a beer to celebrate?"

"Where you going?"

"Woody Creek, probably. Show up if you can stay awake.

I know it's almost your bedtime."

I want to go and be the last man standing to prove him wrong.

Back in the truck, I check my phone and there's a voicemail from Zoe.

Her shaky voice fills the cab.

"I'm so sorry. I'm embarrassed about earlier. I had no idea Neil was in town. He decided to fly in and surprise me based on some stupid advice my dad gave him. Oh, right, yeah, apparently, he's gone out to lunch with my dad at the club. Or they played golf together. I'm not really sure about the details. I do know I'm not going home for Thanksgiving. Or Christmas. Not happening.

"I wanted to leave you a voicemail because this is a lot to type. And I thought if you heard my voice, there won't be room for misinterpretation or confusion."

I don't like the sound of that. *What could I have to be confused about?*

"I escorted Neil to the airport. He's gone. Hopefully for good this time."

Good. I exhale with relief and unclench my fist.

"But—"

She says the words I definitely don't want to hear.

TWENTY-FIVE

ZOE

I'M SITTING IN the backseat of Mara's car in the parking lot at the airport with an eye on the entrance. Neil went through those doors with Jesse and I want to make sure only Jesse comes back out again. After Neil's surprise today, I don't trust him. Because he's a stranger to me.

How does that happen in months after years of being together? Was he always this person and it's taken some distance to see the truth?

If he hasn't changed, this summer I definitely have. Nothing major on paper, but I've given myself permission to explore. To be Zoe. Mildly adventurous, definitely curious, reluctantly independent, I'm not the same woman I was earlier this year.

I thought Neil was my anchor, grounding me. Instead, he was pulling me down, keeping me tethered.

Thankfully, Mara and Mae showed up at the rodeo, with Jesse as backup. I was about to FaceTime Sage again to reinforce to Neil I have zero desire to ever get back together. I'm not sure how effective her yelling at him from my phone screen would've been. Maybe if Lee lurked around in the background flexing muscles or grunting.

The last flight takes off in five minutes. It's not even dark yet and the rodeo is probably just starting.

My mind is still reeling as I sit here, waiting for the jet to taxi down the runway. The whole drive, Neil made his argument while my friends pretended not to be listening. I don't know who I'm more annoyed at: him or my parents. There's no way I'm moving back to Chicago. Hell, I don't want to even visit them. Not for a while.

A text message chirps on my phone. *Justin.*

With a sigh, I rest my head on the back of the front seat.

He's too good to be real. All charm and smarts and kindness and sweet smiles and cocky confidence.

My stomach twists with unwanted realization.

Justin's a wild, untamed fantasy man.

The cowboy on his horse.

If I could invent a man opposite of Neil and the comfortable safety of his upwardly mobile dreams, I couldn't do better than Justin.

And if I'm all about truth and passion, honesty and self, then I'm not being fair to him. Or me.

As the jet engine roars, at the far end of the runway, I open the door and tell the girls I'll be back.

I want to listen to Justin's message in privacy. With my finger over his number, I pause until the plane lifts into the sky. Sitting in the quiet lot, I press call.

My words are rambling and I'm not sure if I'm ever going to get to the point. Or if I have a point.

Clichés like "it's not you, it's me" and "I need time to work on me" float up from my throat and I manage to swallow them before making a complete ass out of myself.

What I don't want to say is we're too different. Or he deserves better. Because even if I'm about as comfortable on a horse as a dog riding a bike, I'm not stupid enough to not want to hold on tight with both hands to a man like Justin.

"Tonight flipped my world. What I thought was over, dead and buried, apparently has a second life sponsored by my parents. I need some time to process. Some space to expel the ghosts.

"I can't go on the trip with you. Not this weekend. It sounds amazing and there's no one I'd rather be alone in the world with than you. But . . ."

Swallowing around the difficult truth of what I need to say, I continue. "It would be easy to continue on like everything is good. You make it so easy to believe life can be simple and good, wild, and free from expectations. With you, it could be right."

I pause again, staring at the phone's counter flip as time passes. "I need a little time."

My eyes fill with tears because this feels like a break up and I'm certain we were only beginning.

"I'm sorry," I whisper as I end the call.

Mara wraps her arms around me from one side and Mae mirrors her pose on the other, sandwiching me between them.

"He's gone," Jesse announces as he joins us by the car.

Tears roll down my cheeks and get lost in the arms around me.

I want to scream about Neil, but I'm crying over Justin.

TWENTY-SIX

ZOE

SUNLIGHT POURS THROUGH the high windows in my little studio at Ashcroft. I'm halfway through my residency and this space feels like home.

The nightmare of Neil's reappearance three weeks ago is beginning to fade as I throw myself into the program. He hasn't reached out again and I haven't returned any of my mother's voicemails.

Studies and inspiration are pinned to an enormous corkboard covering one wall. Pictures of Japanese pottery overflow the designated space, stuck to the walls with blue painter's tape.

A country station on Spotify blasts through my Bluetooth speaker and out the open door. In the background, I can hear a mix of music from the other studios. The warm August day encourages open windows.

Conversation outside ebbs and flows as other artists meander to lunch or over to the kilns. The ranch feels like a mini city, full of life and buzzing energy all focused on creativity.

Tonight I'm firing the first round of pieces for the final show in Denver. I've been creating molds for slip-casting, designing and refining each one until I think my idea will work.

When I'm not working on the final project, I've fallen in love with working on the pottery wheels. Losing myself in the process and being messy, letting my hands create bowls and cups from memory while my mind wanders is good therapy.

Sage should be here any minute. They arrived home from South Africa the same week I started here. I think we were all relieved the dogs and condo survived. Being the nice guy he is, Lee loaded up his Land Rover with my stuff and helped me move into my mini cabin here.

All those people with their tiny home obsessions would be jealous of my place. With enough room to sleep, bathe, and read a book, it defines cozy.

I no longer feel homeless and lost.

"Knock, knock," Sage says as she walks into the studio.

Out of habit, I wipe my hands on the back of my overalls even though I haven't been working with wet clay this afternoon.

I give her a big hug, enveloping my sprite-sized bestie whose head comes up to my shoulder.

Squeezing me back, she says, "I've missed you. You're too far away."

"Says the person who left me for a month to go to the other side of the world."

"Good point. And that leads me to my brilliant idea I had while driving over here."

"Uh oh. I never trust the ideas you get while behind the wheel."

"This one's good. You're going to rent Lee's condo. I won the coin flip and we're moving into mine. There's no one else I'd rather live next door to than you. We can meet on the front steps for coffee every morning."

"Pretty soon it's going to start snowing. I love you and your crazy, but I'm not sitting in snow with you to drink coffee."

She hops up on the workbench next to me. "Fine, we can trade off sitting in each other's kitchens."

"I can't afford the rent on either of your places."

"Pfft. Pay what you paid with . . . before." Her nose crinkles with disgust.

"Neil. We can say his name. Doesn't give him any power."

"I'd prefer not to. I can't believe we were so wrong about him for so long."

"I think he changed. I know I have." For the better, I hope. "He's not a terrible person. As far as I know he doesn't kill small animals or fund hate groups."

"As far as you know." She sounds unconvinced.

"He's no Landon. You know, he hit on me when I was buying my sad cake?"

"Nice change of subject back to the barnacle on my past love life."

I give her a grin. "We've all made mistakes when it comes to love."

Sage presses her lips together and squints at me, but doesn't speak.

"What?" I finally ask when I blink and lose the staring contest.

"You know what. Or who."

With a sigh, I ignore her. My glazes and silver powder for the next step in my project require my attention right this very moment. Unfortunately, they're all perfectly organized.

"I haven't spoken to Justin."

"How long are you going to pretend you're fine without him?"

"As long as it takes for me to prove to myself I don't need a man to complete me?" I barely meet her eyes, the words sounding silly in my own ears.

"Don't let the calf get away because you're afraid to use

your rope," she says and frowns. "I don't think that works as a metaphor."

"I think you want the one about getting back in the saddle."

"I'm not talking about random sex. Although at this point it wouldn't be random, would it?" Her voice goes soft.

Stupid tears multiply in my eyes. "No, not random at all. It's too soon to fall in love with another man."

Her laughter fills the room. "Question answered."

"Shut up."

"Can't stop, won't stop." Grinning, she bobs her head. "Where is the cowboy this week?"

Justin's been busy. Or he's giving me space. Or he's moved on. If I tell her, I'll be admitting I'm tracking the rodeo circuit. "Wyoming yesterday."

"How long a drive is it?" She swings her slim legs back and forth, letting her feet bump the counter.

"I'm not going to chase down a cowboy like a horny buckle bunny. I mean, I get the appeal. Who can resist the allure of shiny metal *right there*?" I point at my crotch, in case Sage has forgotten where a belt buckle would be. *"Right there."*

"Tell that to your rodeo man." She points behind me.

I spin around so fast I almost trip. When I see the empty doorway, relief and disappointment mix together.

"I hate you."

"You have your answer." Hopping off the counter, she grins. "My work here is done. Where's lunch?"

Ashcroft's dining room is open to the public for lunch several times a week and for dinner on Saturday night. A local chef prepares seasonal farm to table food for the artists and visitors. Everything is amazing, because this place is heaven.

Inside the large, open space, most of the tables are already full of people. Normally, I grab a tray to go through the line and find an empty seat. By now, friendships are beginning to form among the residents.

"If you want to get your food, I'll stake out a place to sit," I tell Sage, already moving into the maze of tables while I scan for empty seats or finished plates of food.

At a round table in the corner, Emily Mays holds court. Surrounding her, and hanging on her every word, is a group of visitors. Most are middle aged or older, and everyone is nicely dressed in a casual way only money can achieve—unlike the resident artists, who are a hot mess in work clothes covered in the debris of creativity.

Spotting me, Emily waves me over to her table. "Here's Zoe Saragossa, one of our most talented artists in residence this summer."

Ah, the group is probably donors or patrons, as Emily likes to label them. Deep pockets and a passion for supporting the arts make me being here possible.

With a friendly smile, I sweep a hand over my messy bun and dirty overalls. I'm definitely not dressed to impress, but I do look the part of crazy artist.

I greet Emily and nod at the well-preserved faces staring up at me. "I hope you're having a lovely lunch."

A few murmur their appreciation of the food while others observe me like I'm a colorful bird at the zoo.

"Let me introduce you," Emily says, touching my wrist. She rattles off each name.

I nod. Smile. Nod. These could be potential collectors of my work, but it's likely I'll never see any of them again.

"And finally, our patron and one of our founders, Felecia Garrison."

At the familiar name, my eyes lock on the silver-haired woman in the huge antique Navajo turquoise necklace and crisp, white linen shirt. She's the most impeccable of all. Deep, soulful eyes like Justin's stare back at me.

A man holding a tray of desserts weaves his way over to us. In his dark, fitted collared shirt, I assume he's a waiter because he's dressed in the typical uniform.

"It's lovely to meet you . . ." My focus shifts to the waiter with the cake slices. " . . . BB."

Somehow I keep smiling while inside my pulse feels like I'm hiking up Ajax mountain. My breath goes shallow. I press my fingers against the center of my chest before my heart can beat its way through the bones encasing it. He's not supposed to be here.

"Why are you pretending to be a waiter?" I try to make sense of his appearance. "Wait, are you really a waiter and not a cowboy?"

The ladies at the table titter at my mistake. One of them asks, "Who's BB?"

"Me." Justin's warm, brown eyes spark with amusement and his full lips curve into a small smile. "I'm having lunch with my grandmother."

My attention settles on the older woman. Definitely the same eyes and the same warmth behind them.

Justin hands me a plate. "Did you sense the cake? You can have mine."

"Oh, I couldn't." We both know I could and would if I weren't standing in front of the director and patrons.

"It's so nice to meet you, too, Zoe." Mrs. Garrison's voice breaks my cake and cowboy haze. "I look forward to seeing your work. Emily's had nothing but wonderful things to say about the project. You're using *kintsugi* techniques?"

To compose myself enough to speak coherently, I force air deep into my lungs. "Thank you. I'm going to be firing several pieces tonight. Wish me luck."

Justin's grandmother's gaze shifts between him and me, her clever eyes observing us carefully.

"Something tells me you don't need luck when it comes to going after what you want."

Her words click, and suddenly my being here doesn't feel as serendipitous as a last minute cancelation. Justin being related to one of the founders can't be coincidence. Interesting how he left off that part when I mentioned Ashcroft over dinner.

My hands dampen. I have the same feeling as I did in the fourth grade spelling bee when I knew I misspelled conspiracy.

How did I miss this connection? And why didn't Justin tell me?

"Care to join us? Apparently, we have enough cake for everyone." Emily nods at Justin, who stands close to me.

"Thank you for the invitation. I'm here with a friend and we've just arrived." I set down the tainted cake. Rejecting cake goes against my fundamental beliefs. I fake a smile at the important people. "My door is open this afternoon if anyone would like to stop by. I'm always happy to talk about my project."

Emily gives me a look of motherly approval while Felecia Garrison studies her grandson.

After saying good-bye, I step away from the table, already searching for Sage in the buffet line. I think we should skip lunch.

"I'll be right back," Justin tells the table behind me. "Need to return the tray."

I speed up, almost racing through the large round tables in my own version of a barrel race.

"Zoe, wait." His scent of fresh cut grass and leather wraps around me like a lasso.

"Not here," I whisper through my teeth. Spotting Sage, I point behind me and then out the door while making a drinking gesture. I hope she understands crazy charades.

Once we're outside, Justin catches up and matches his stride to mine.

"It's good to see you." From the corner of my eye, I see his happy smile.

"Why didn't you tell me? I'm an idiot. What did you have to do to get me a spot here? Donate money? Promise to give them all ponies?" I continue stomping in the direction of my studio. "I feel like the biggest fool."

Flinging open my screen door, I dash inside before it slams behind me. The satisfying smack of wood against the frame doesn't come. Because Justin stands in the doorway.

"I should've told you. I'd planned to come clean on the trail ride. Before you started here." He steps inside and softly closes the door, then leans his back against the wall with his arms folded

He's smart to stay over there. I need space. Right now, I don't know if I want to cry or break things. I pick up a small sculpture and throw it at the wall. The piece creates a satisfying crack at impact. Three pieces now exist where there was one.

Tears fill my eyes and my chin wobbles. "I didn't earn my spot. I felt like an imposter standing in front of Emily and the donors. I need to resign."

"Hold on one damn second." He lifts his hands, palms facing me. "You're making a big leap based on assumptions, assigning blame where there's only correlation."

Crossing my arms, I lean against my workbench.

"Yes, I thought about making a call. But I didn't. No, I didn't pull strings to get you a spot here. Nor did I beg or force Emily to extend an invitation. And if you think I bribed someone to drop out, I didn't do that either. You earned this position with your talent and perseverance. People who know more about contemporary art recognize your talent."

He pushes off the wall and slowly stalks toward me. The pure masculine energy rolling off of him reminds me of a bull. I'm the bullfighter. He steps closer and I press against the bench, no place to escape unless I dash across the room.

"I'm giving you space and time, but I'm not going to allow you to invent reasons to push me away. Your face lit up when you spoke about Ashcroft. This is where you're supposed to be. Now you're vibrating with happiness. Or at least you were until you spotted me." He stops within a few feet of me. "You can be mad at me. You can tell me you don't ever want to see me again, but there's no chance I'm going to watch you throw away your dreams because you don't like having a fairy godmother. Or in my case, a fairy cowboy."

My mouth twists into a smile.

He rolls his eyes. "That's a horrible description, but I stand by my point. Supporting your dreams makes me happy. Your happiness matters to me."

"Thank you," I manage to say, my voice barely above a whisper.

His brows lower for a second before he flattens his expression. "You're welcome."

Commence the awkward staring contest.

"That's it?" he lowers his voice and the crease reappears on his forehead.

I stall for time. "I'm processing."

"Mind if I look around while you decide I'm not an asshole? I've been curious to see what comes out of that mind of yours. Promise you won't throw anything at my head?"

"Go ahead." I sweep my arm around the space. "I guess I owe you."

He takes another step closer to me. "You owe me nothing. You earned this."

My skin pebbles in the wake of his touch on my arm.

"There is something I want." His eyes hold an unexpected nervousness.

"What?" My voice is nothing more than a breath.

"I want a chance with you."

When I try to inhale, my breath sticks in my throat.

"If you're not ready, I'll wait. But you should know, I'm not a patient man. Not in my nature to not go after what I want. However, if you say no, I'll respect that, and walk away."

"Who are you?" I'm not sure what I'm asking, but once again, I can't believe he's real.

"Simple cowboy who really likes this super cool artist who's also one of the most beautiful and strongest women I've ever met."

"Thank you for the compliment." I dip my chin and stare at him. "That's about me. Tell me who you are."

"I forgot feisty." He leans against the work table across from me. "Okay, I'm a son without a father, a brother to sisters, a grandson to a matriarch. I'm competitive and stubborn. Most of the time I don't like people and prefer my own company.

"Let's see." He runs an index finger over his chin in the dip below his bottom lip. "If you want my résumé, I studied finance at CU and have an MBA from Stanford. I manage the Garrison family trust, as well as the day-to-day operations of the ranch."

"Finance? MBA?" I definitely wasn't expecting that.

"I know. I don't seem the type. But I'll show you the diplomas if you want."

"I believe you." Uncrossing my arms, I rest my hands next to my hips. "Anything else?"

"I have a pretty nice condo in Denver, but I rarely stay there. My family uses it more than I do."

"So not just a country mouse after all?"

"The city has some good things. In small doses."

"I agree."

"See? Another thing we have in common." I like the way his shy smile feels like a secret he shares only with me.

"Am I forgiven for meddling? I promise I'm not trying to

control your life like some weird puppet master."

What life?

"Earlier this year, I was on cruise control. In the small span of time I've known you, I don't feel like I'm an observer anymore. For the first time in a long time, I feel alive. Because of you. I'm not mad about your involvement in Ashcroft, I'm stunned. You barely know me."

He closes the space between us. "Time doesn't determine how well we know a person. We can spend years working with someone and barely scratch deeper than the superficial bullshit we all present to the world. Or we can meet someone and see a spark in them that makes us want to know more. To know everything."

He's a cowboy philosopher-business-whiz-buckle-hoarding fantasy come to life.

"And what do you want?" *Please say me.*

He stares at my mouth for a beat before answering. "I'm dying to kiss you."

"Please." I barely finish the word when he's in front of me, his hand cupping my cheek.

"Zoe," his breath co-mingles with mine as he whispers my name with reverence and hope, "I'll do anything for you."

When he softly presses his mouth to mine, it's unexpected. There's no crashing of lips against teeth or impatience. He kisses me like a man who has all the time in the world to fall in love and he's going to enjoy every single second.

"Am I forgiven?" he whispers along my neck when we come up for air.

"No more surprises?" My voice is breathless. Tilting my head, I give him more access to my skin.

"Now where's the fun in life without the unexpected?" His teeth nip the tender spot where neck becomes shoulder.

A shiver runs down my spine in response to his touch.

"Does your studio door have a lock?" he asks with a needy rasp.

"Yes." I slip away from him to close it. I loop the hook for the screen door, too.

Justin eyes the cluttered space. "Not ideal, but we can make this work."

I lift my eyebrows in question.

He meets me in the middle of the space. With his hands on my upper arms, he slowly guides me to the old Victorian settee underneath the giant pin board. Wrapping his arms around my back, he kisses me slow and deep until my knees weaken. I slide down to the settee's worn velvet cushion, pulling him along with me. My head rests on the curved arm and he stretches his body over mine.

Settling between my legs, he braces some of his weight on his thighs and props his hand next to my head. I widen my thighs, and he grinds against my center. Lifting my left leg, he props it on the back of the sofa.

All the while, his lips never leave my skin. He alternates between deep, soul kisses and trailing his mouth along my jaw and neck. The tender softness behind my ears becomes one of his favorite places to lick. My toes curl and my back arches with each pass of his tongue.

I thought his kisses were deliberate before. Today I realize how painstakingly cautious he's been. The man has been holding back. Because sweet mother of pearl buttons, I've never been kissed like this. I feel worshipped.

He shifts his weight, allowing his hand to cup and squeeze my breast. The contact cracks through my last inhibitions. I need him and I need him now.

Resolved, I gently push him off me.

"Do you want to stop?" he asks, his lips darkened from our kisses and his eyes even darker with desire.

"Hell no." I flip the buttons on my overalls and slip out of them. Next I peel my tank over my head, leaving me only in my pink bra and mismatched teal underwear.

His eyes widen and then he grins in the most wicked, mischievous way. "Can you be quiet?"

"Give me a second." I scramble out from under him. Letting my overalls flop to the floor, I dash to the work bench. In a few seconds, music fills the room.

Justin stands to meet me. Stepping into his arms, I immediately go for the hem of his shirt. Pulling it out of his dress pants, my fingers sweep over the warm, smooth skin of his abs.

He's already unbuttoning his shirt from the top while I undo his belt.

"Why do you have so many buttons on your clothes?" My fingers twist with his as I race to get him naked like my life depends on it.

"I'm adding impatience to the ever growing list of things we have in common." He gives up trying to remove his own clothes and instead focuses on my bra.

With a flick of his thumb, my bra's clasp falls open. The last button of his shirt is undone and I sweep my hands over his chest, shoving the fabric down his shoulders. Where it catches on his wrists.

"More damn buttons?"

He exhales a chuckle while sliding the pink lace cups of my bra away from my breasts. "You had a head start."

We're both naked from the waist up. A sigh escapes my lips the first moment our skin touches when he envelops me in his arms again.

His tongue strokes mine as his thumbs hook into the sides of my underwear. I hum into his mouth while my own hands slide his pants over his hips.

"Boots," he says and it sounds a little like boobs.

"Huh?" I mumble against his mouth.

"Boots have to come off before pants." He holds my shoulders and steps back. His mouth curves into a satisfied grin as he observes me, naked before him for the first time. "How'd I get so lucky?"

Quickly and gracefully, he removes his boots, jeans, and finally his boxers. Every inch of naked Justin is perfect. I take a moment to stare at him, letting my eyes sweep over each ridge of strong muscle. Lighter brown hair darkens as it trails down from his chest past his navel.

What I imagined and dreamed about since the first time I saw him in chaps doesn't disappoint. He's long and hard. Beautiful.

I reach for his cock, gliding my hand along his smooth length. His groan encourages me and I tighten my grip.

"You're so beautiful," he whispers right before pressing his lips to mine.

We tumble on the settee, a tangle of limbs and hands exploring new skin while we kiss and nip. He's everything I imagined. Each touch is reverent and deliberate. Soft strokes become focused, and soon I'm arching into the waves of pleasure his fingers pull from my body.

I don't think I've ever come so quickly.

"I love that." His voice holds awe. He kisses over the swell of one breast as he slowly continues to slide his fingers inside of me. "Shall we go for another?"

My answer is a searing kiss, because honestly, I'm not sure I'm capable of speech. He hums against my mouth before sliding down my body. Kneeling on the floor, he shifts my body and lifts my calves to his shoulders.

When his tongue makes contact with the most intimate part of me, my eyes close and I grapple to dig my fingers into the soft velvet cushion.

I forget to be quiet. I forget where we are.

The world ceases to exist outside this room as pleasure begins to pulse low in my abdomen. My thighs tighten around his head as my body tenses. A few more strokes of his fingers and a soft suck with his mouth, and I shatter into nothing but blissful sensation.

His kiss to my inner thigh grounds me, bringing me back down to earth.

"I believe good things happen in threes." He grins at me from his spot between my legs.

"I'm not sure I can handle more."

"Want to find out? You'll never know unless you try." He strokes his erection, fisting the tip.

"I want to, I really do, but I don't have any condoms."

"A cowboy is always prepared." He stands and searches for his wallet. Finding the foil packet, he holds it up in question. "Are you sure?"

My answer is to lie back against the cushion and pull him over me. When he's ready, I take him in my hand, brushing his tip against my sensitive bundle of nerves. My body jerks in response.

"I thought you were beautiful before, but nothing compares to the sight of you now." His finger caresses my cheek and then down my neck to my breast, where he circles my nipple. "You have the loveliest flush on your skin, and there's a passion in your eyes that's never been there before. I want to see you like this every day. I want to be the reason you radiate joy."

As if his words aren't enough to incinerate me, he slides inside of me, inch by slow inch until he fills me. We're joined together into one. The weight of the moment hits me and I blink away unexpected tears.

"Anything for you," he whispers against my lips, stealing my answer with his kiss.

I keep my eyes open, staring into the warmth of his. Pure happiness reflects back at me as we move together.

When I feel the pull of another orgasm, I close my eyes and tuck my head into his shoulder. He bends my knee, changing our angle as he brings himself closer to the edge.

I open my eyes again as my body reaches a new peak. His face twists with ecstasy as his movements still and he erupts.

Our panting becomes steady breaths. He rests his head on my shoulder while I trace circles and curves on his back, his warmth covering me.

He must be able to feel the racing of my heart beneath his cheek. It flutters around the cage of my ribs, full of joy and new love.

"Looks like Zoe's not in her studio after all. Oh well. We should come back later when she's back." Sage's loud voice on the other side of the door breaks me out of the post sex haze. We're naked in my studio and not an hour ago I invited everyone to come check out my work.

"Expecting company?" Justin's sleepy voice asks near my ear.

"Only your grandmother and the rest of the board."

He jumps off the settee, and I laugh as his still semi-hard cock bounces in the air.

"Are we in trouble?" I giggle.

"You made sure the door's locked, right?"

I nod. "The windows are high enough you'd have to jump or stand on something to see in. Plus, Sage is running interference from the sound of it."

Panic leaves his face. "Good. We should still probably get dressed and be presentable."

"And light a candle. I think it probably smells like sex in here."

With a happy smirk on his face, he picks up his pants. "I'm sure we're not the first to have sex in one of these spaces."

"I'm not a performance artist, so let's keep this to ourselves, k?" I look around the floor for my underwear. Lying next to it are the shattered pieces of the slip-cast heart I threw earlier. A new idea floats into my head for my project.

"If we go on the trail ride, there won't be any interruptions." He hands me my bra. "There are benefits to being alone in the wilderness with me."

I narrow my eyes at him.

"Come on, say yes and you won't regret it." He leans over to kiss me.

"Yes."

I'm hopelessly falling for this cowboy.

And it's the best adventure I've ever been on.

TWENTY-SEVEN

JUSTIN

ZOE'S AN AMAZING artist, but she's a terrible actress.

When I shared my weekend getaway idea with her at the rodeo, her face looked like she'd sucked on a lemon. I struggled to keep a straight face as she pretended a backcountry trail ride sounded fun.

Yet when I brought it up again at Ashcroft last week, she agreed to an overnight trip. Post sex endorphins can make people agree to crazy things.

I shouldn't be amused by her reaction, but I am. And because she's such a trooper, I'm going to make it a weekend she'll never forget.

If she said "No, let's spend a weekend in bed in a five star hotel in Denver," I'd have made the reservations that night.

Maybe I'll bring her to Denver soon to make it up to her. We can stay in the condo for the Ashcroft show in October.

If this whole surprise doesn't backfire in a glorious mess right in my face.

On the surface, Zoe and I are going to be roughing it. Tent, bedrolls, sleeping bags, and some freeze dried meals. I'll bring my rod and impress her with my fly fishing skills as I catch dinner for us.

I'm pulling out all the stops on this cowboy fantasy fulfillment.

To her delight, I involve Tammy in the planning. She's more than happy to fuss over me and give her unsolicited advice on the dos and don'ts of courting a woman.

"If she's still speaking to you, you need to pay her lots of compliments. And not just about how pretty she is or how much you like her breasts. Women like to hear what else you admire besides the packaging. We may tend to be vain, but we're also aware that the exterior is subject to change. Flatter her mind and honor her soul."

I nod in agreement with her words.

"Good. You're listening. That's key."

"You should write a book, Tammy."

"What do I know about love? Three strikes and I'm out." She wipes her hands on a towel. "Damn buttercream is messy business."

I drive into town to pick up Zoe as the sun begins to crest the mountains. Sprinkled on the slopes, one or two aspen trees shimmer with golden leaves amongst the green. Soon frost will dust the ground in the mornings as summer fades into fall.

Next to me I have large coffees for both of us and a couple of donuts from City Market. Yes, they're bribery for the early hour.

We have six hours of riding ahead of us and I want to get to our destination with time to enjoy the evening before dark.

Cash, one of my favorite trail horses, and Dolly, are loaded in the trailer. We'll park at the trailhead and someone from the ranch will come collect the truck and bring it to the other end for us tomorrow. We could ride both directions, but Zoe's a novice and I don't want to overdo it.

In the past week, she's been up to the ranch for riding lessons a couple more times. I'm confident Dolly will take good care of her.

Seeing Zoe's face when my surprise is revealed will be worth all the duplicity.

When she answers the door, she's mid-yawn. "Sorry. I'm not a morning person."

"I have coffee and donuts in the truck."

"Why are we lingering around here?" She grins and gives me a quick kiss. "I didn't know what to pack, so I only have this little bag."

"You're not going to need much. We're only gone tonight." And I plan for us to be naked most of the night.

"So the two pairs of heels and the little black dress I packed will be too much?"

I almost miss the curb. "You're kidding, right?"

"I am. It's mostly extra socks and warm, cozy things in case it's freezing."

"I promise I'll keep you warm." I envelop her in my arms from behind. "The best part of camping is spooning for warmth."

"I've always wondered what the appeal is." Turning in my embrace, she faces me. Doubt fills her eyes.

"Trust me, I'm going to change your mind." I brush my lips against hers.

"I trust you'll give it your best effort." She wrinkles her nose and I kiss that, too.

The trail is easy, in spite of the gain in altitude and winding switchbacks. We climb up out of the Roaring Fork Valley, heading east toward the Continental Divide. As the hours pass, we fall into a rhythm on our horses. Cash and I lead while Dolly happily follows behind us. At times conversation is impossible because of the terrain. Other areas of the path allow us to ride side by side.

I check in frequently, making sure Zoe is doing okay.

"The view is incredible. I feel like we're explorers and the first people to ever see these mountains."

"It's rare to find a place where you don't see constant reminders of humans and our impact." Other than the trail, there is no evidence of modern society. No cell phone towers or overhead electrical wires. No roads or buildings. Just us and the horses.

Cash carries our supplies in two saddlebags flanking his belly. Zoe's small pack easily fits into one of the larger bags. Our bedrolls are tied behind my saddle and hers. I also have a tent.

The trail winds through a grove of trees right before opening into a wide, green valley flanked on one side by scree slides.

"Okay, now I feel like I'm on another planet. I've never seen anything like this." Zoe's voice holds awe as she turns her head to take in the view.

"Just wait. It gets better."

"Stop. That's impossible. I'm not sure I can handle more natural beauty. This is all part of your ploy to get me to be happy about sleeping on the ground, isn't it?"

"Is it working?" I pull Cash beside Dolly so I can see Zoe's expression. Even in the shadow of the brim of her straw hat and her sunglasses, her face glows with happiness.

"Maybe. For now. I'm still not sure I'm up for anything where my food and deodorant have to be stored in a can because of bears. Bears who might try to eat my head while I'm sleeping."

"You're adorable."

"Are you really going to fish for our dinner?" She dips her head to look at me over the top of her sunglasses.

"I can."

"That's sexy."

I chuckle and give her a wicked grin. "Good to know. Ready for lunch?"

"Starved. How can sitting on a horse make me so hungry?"

I spot a location on flat ground near some trees where we can tie up the horses. There's grass for them to chomp on and a narrow stream for water. I help Zoe down from Dolly. When she's steady on the ground, I give her a lingering kiss.

"Can I help?" she asks after we break apart.

"No, I've got it." I loop and knot both sets of reins around a pair of narrow aspen trunks. In one of Cash's saddle bags, I locate the picnic supplies.

"Here, you can spread the blanket."

"Did you make all this?" Laying down the faded quilt made from old jeans, Zoe eyes the food I'm unpacking.

I laugh. "Tammy's doing. She and the kitchen staff make all the food for the ranch hands and our trail rides."

"She's the ranch mom, isn't she?"

"Exactly." Kneeling, I open the containers of various salads and set the steak sandwiches on the quilt. "She's outdone herself. I think she wants me to impress you."

Zoe picks up her sandwich and takes a huge bite. After chewing, she moans and swallows. "Consider me impressed. This is amazing."

Relieved she likes it, I relax on the ground next to her. Stretching out my legs, I watch her enjoy lunch.

"Taking in the view?" she asks as she spears a chunk of watermelon with her fork.

"It's beautiful."

"You're not even facing the valley."

"My view is better." I grin at her. "Trust me. I've been coming to these mountains my whole life."

"You're lucky, you realize this, right?"

"I do. I never take any of this for granted." I eat my own

food as we fall into silence.

The wind rustles the small aspen leaves and in the distance a hawk whistles, circling its prey. The small creek splashes and gurgles over rocks as it winds through the valley.

After removing her hat and sunglasses, Zoe stretches out beside me and rests her head on my thigh. "Thank you."

"Good food?"

"I'll be sure to write Tammy a card, but I was saying thank you for today. For bringing me up here and sharing this with me." Twisting her head, she stares into my eyes. "I think this might be my favorite day."

"It's not over yet." My fingers brush over her silky braid.

"How do you do it?" she murmurs, sounding sleepy.

"Hmm?" Shifting my body, I bring her closer so she rests her head on my chest. My arm slides under her shoulder and curls around her waist.

"Live in the moment."

Sun warms our skin as we cuddle. Sliding my hand down her arm, I list some of my truths. "Lots of practice. Accepting what I can and can't change. Knowing who I am helps."

"Who is Justin Garrison?"

"I'm still finding out. Cowboy is the obvious label, but I run a business and I'm responsible for dozens of people's livelihood. I feel responsible for my family. Probably because my dad was a narcissist who only cared about himself. Never, and I mean, never, do I want to go down the same path he did. Although for a few years after college, I was a selfish, egotistical prick."

She giggles and rests her chin on my chest. "Really?"

"That's funny to you?"

"I can see it. It's surprising you're not more of a cocky prick."

I run my finger over her forehead and follow her hairline to her jaw. "I made a promise to myself to not take the easy path through life. It would be easy to walk away from the ranch, stop competing. Get a job focused on making money and let life carry me along."

As we stare into each other's eyes, I see tears form in the corners of hers. When one falls, I brush it away with the pad of my thumb. "Why are you crying?"

"Because that life you describe is the one we're all supposed to want. The American Dream."

"And you don't want that either?"

"I want a partner and a family of my own, but the rest of it feels like a box I'm being shoved into. It feels suffocating."

"Get out of the box. We get one wild life to follow our dreams. The longer we wait, the more we end up trying to live up to other people's expectations."

She scoots closer and sweeps her lips over mine in a light kiss. Falling into the feeling of her lying on top of me, our bodies pressed together and our mouths exploring, I close my eyes. Lost in our kiss.

This feels right.

Like truly wild things, it's beautiful and fragile.

"I could stay here all afternoon, but if we do, we won't get to our destination by nightfall."

"Why can't we camp here?" Her lips skim my jaw.

"Because I have a plan."

"What happened to living free of expectations?"

I poke her nose. "Trust me, you'll like the other location even more than this."

"Okay, let's giddy up and go."

Instead of releasing her, I roll on top of her, pinning her arms above her head. Giving her one more deep kiss, I slowly grind my hips into hers. "I'd stay here and make love to you all afternoon, but you're going to be happier if we wait."

Her eyes slowly blink before they close. "You can't say things like that. It's not fair."

"I never said I was fair." Shifting my weight, I kneel between her legs. I take a moment to memorize how beautiful she is. Her dark braid has come loose and her golden skin glows in the dappled light coming through the full aspen trees.

An unfamiliar tightness grips my chest as emotion floods my body. What started as playful curiosity and casual interest is changing into something more, something deeper.

I'm not willing to label or closely examine this new feeling just yet. With a deep inhale, I expand my chest, making more room in my heart for Zoe.

TWENTY-EIGHT

ZOE

I NEVER WANT to leave our lunch spot. Justin has to bribe me with an extra brownie and the promise of something even better to get me back on Dolly.

The afternoon ride takes us over another pass and through thick forests. Sunlight warms my skin and I strip off my shirt, riding in only my yoga camisole. The thin interlaced straps on the back may give me weird tan lines, but the sun and breeze feel amazing.

Dolly's a trooper. We fall into an easy partnership and she follows Cash without much coaxing or direction from me. My nerves fade the longer I ride until being on her back feels comfortable. I can't believe in such a short time I've fallen in love with riding.

The man ahead of me is to blame for that. I've spent most of the ride staring at his back. Watching the roll of his hips as he sits in the saddle has me occasionally squeezing my own thighs. Which sometimes means Dolly takes off in a trot until I can slow her down again. It's a good thing Justin doesn't realize our inability to maintain a steady pace is due to my lusting after his backside.

I'm having a serious relationship with his broad shoulders and narrow waist. In a white T-shirt that looks like it may have shrunk a little in the wash, his back muscles taunt me. Close, but not close enough to run my hands over them.

In other words, for hours I'm being tortured by his proximity.

The sun slides lower in the sky behind us as we ride east. The trail twists up a slope, revealing a view of sharp peaks in the distance. A few have traces of glacial snow despite months of summer.

"Our spot is over this ridge."

While I've loved being out here in the middle of nowhere and the amazing views, and making out in a valley with Justin, I'm ready to not be straddling a horse. I'd rather straddle a cowboy.

We cross the high point in the trail and begin to descend into another narrow valley. Somewhere close, a stream rushes down the mountain. It's the only sound beside birdsong and the clop of the horses' hooves on the rocks scattered over the trail. The late afternoon sun casts long shadows.

Justin stops and dismounts. I glance around at the level spot as he leads Cash to another grove of aspens.

"This is it?" Ahead of us the trail takes a sharp turn and disappears.

"You sound disappointed. Wait until you see the stars tonight. It's clear enough the Milky Way should be spectacular."

The city girl in me balks at camping on the side of a mountain. All day I've convinced myself I can do this. Push myself out of my comfort zone and have a new adventure. This is what I came here for, right?

After semi-gracefully sliding down from Dolly's back, I lead her over to the trees. My euphoria from earlier fades as I absorb the reality we're going to be sleeping in a nylon bag on the ground. I didn't even camp as a kid. My mother is allergic to the outdoors.

I really have to pee. Staring at the flat grass and open pattern of trees, I wonder where exactly I'm supposed to go.

Justin looks so happy, grinning at me and chatting away to the horses as he removes their saddles and tack. He slips off the bridles and replaces them with more comfortable harnesses with longer leads.

I can do this. It's one night.

But what if this is what he wants to do all the time? If I don't speak up, I'm not being true to either of us. Trapped again by trying to please him to my own detriment.

"I can't."

"What can't you do?" His dark eyes meet mine and there's amusement in them as he steps closer.

"The camping and sleeping in a tent. I'm sorry. I should've said something earlier. It's not dark yet, can we keep riding? Can horses ride at night? I'm sorry. I don't even know if they have night vision. That's probably dangerous."

"Shh," he hushes me.

"I've ruined everything." Tears swell in my eyes. "I should've told you before. I'm not this kind of woman."

"What kind is that?" He brushes away a few escaped tears from my cheeks. "Beautiful and adventurous? Open to trying new things and going outside of your comfort zone? Because you're all of the above."

"I'm not. I like hotels and room service. Flushable toilets with seats. Chairs. Walls. Windows. Screens. Air conditioning. Pillows. A bed." I list random things I suddenly can't live without. "And I really need to pee, but there's no privacy."

His lips form a straight line, and I can't tell if he's fighting laughter or disappointment.

"Why didn't you say something earlier?" His voice lacks the disappointment I'm expecting.

"I was hoping for a miracle?" Talking isn't helping me forget my bladder is about to revolt. I bounce from foot to foot to distract myself.

Soft laughter spills out of him. "Come on, I'll show you."

"Can't you point me in the direction?" When I agreed to this I never thought about how to handle simple biological functions in the woods. My mind was too full of sexy thoughts about making love under the stars or in fields full of wildflowers.

Thanks for ruining my fantasies, reality.

Justin holds out his hand for me. "I know the perfect spot right around the bend in the trail."

"Seems a little far."

"With bears and other wildlife in the area, best to keep things separate."

"Not comforting."

"You're stuck with me tonight. I promise I won't let anything happen to you."

Instead of watching my footing, I allow myself to stare at his face. I see nothing but earnest honesty. He's too good to be true. Too bad I'm not the right kind of woman for him. At least we'll have tonight together.

"We're here," he announces.

I drag my eyes away from his and look around for the promised privacy.

"What's that?" I point at the small log cabin perched on the hill a few yards away.

He squeezes my hand. "I'd never make you sleep in a tent. Do you like it?"

"You see it, too? It's real?" I've never been so relieved to see a house in my life.

"It is. Bathroom is the second door on the right."

When I start jogging toward the door, I don't even know if it's locked. Thankfully, it's not. Inside, I barely notice anything but the open door to the bathroom. With a deep sigh,

I finally release my bladder and observe the small room. An antler-framed mirror reflects the light from the window. A small vanity and sink take up the wall opposite the toilet. I expect bare bones, like a hunting cabin, but the fixtures and lighting are nice.

Washing my hands, I cringe when I see a streak of dirt on my face. I say a silent thank you to the hot water and the promise of a hot shower soon.

On the other side of the door, Justin's boots clomp down the hall and then heavy bags drop on the wood floor.

I peek my head into the hallway and follow the sound of him moving around the living area. When I reach the end of the hall, my jaw falls open.

The far wall is all glass, facing an interrupted view of mountain peaks and valleys straight out of a painting. A large deck juts off the house, seeming to float above the sloping valley. Drawn to the vista outside, I pass through a living room with nice yet comfortable furniture and a large fieldstone fireplace on one wall.

Somewhere beyond those sharp mountains, the rest of the world churns on. People go to Walmart and the movies, make dinner, pray for bedtime for their kids, and complain about the grind of life. Somewhere out there is reality, full of expectations and disappointment.

"Better than sleeping on the ground?" Justin steps next to me. In his hands are two ice cold bottles of beer, small drops of condensation already forming and gliding down the necks.

"Where did those come from?" I accept one of the beers and then take a long sip of the crisp IPA.

"House has running water and a kitchen. All propane or solar powered." He grins, revealing those beautiful white teeth of his. He turns me by placing a hand on my shoulder.

"Holy crack." The simple kitchen is outfitted with all the

basics, but my attention focuses on a large glass cake stand holding a chocolate frosted cake. "There's cake?"

"I guessed about the flavor." The sweet earnest expression is back in his eyes when I face him. He wants to make me happy.

"You made a cake for me?" I'm stunned.

He brushes a hand over his head, a shy smile on his face. "Lord, no. You don't want my cooking. Tammy's responsible."

"How'd you get it here? In your pack?"

"Well . . ." Taking my hand, he leads me to the kitchen sink. "Don't get mad."

"I'm not sure I've forgiven you yet for leading me to think I was going to be sleeping in a tent tonight."

"Then since you're already mad, look out the window."

I'm not sure what I'm supposed to see. There's a small barn surrounded by a simple wood fence next to the cabin. "The horses don't have to sleep outside either?"

"Unlike someone else, they don't mind sleeping outdoors."

"What am I supposed to notice?" I stare out the window.

Stepping behind me, so close I can feel the warmth from his chest brush against my back, he lifts his hand and points toward the trees.

"Is that a road?"

I both feel and hear his deep chuckle.

"You're telling me we could drive here?" I try to turn around but his hips pin mine to the counter and his arms create a cage around me.

"You'd need an off road Jeep to traverse the fire road."

"But it's possible?" I ask, disbelieving this magical place can be accessed by something as basic as a Jeep.

He sweeps my braid away from my neck and trails his nose from my ear to the curve of my shoulder. "Didn't you have fun today?"

Thinking about our picnic and the slow, carefree pace of

the trip here, I nod.

"Good." His mouth slowly follows the same path as his nose.

My body hums with pleasure while my mind attempts to process the how, why, and where.

"What is this place?" I ask, tilting my head to the side to give him more access to my new favorite spot.

"A family property. Originally my father had it built for my mother, but now it's part of the 10th Mountain hut system when we're not using it."

"It's incredible. Anyone can come here?"

"We screen the renters. In the winter, it's accessible by skis. During the summer, we use it for overnight trail rides. Sometimes I come up here to get away."

"From the ranch?"

"From people in general."

"Not a lover of humans?"

"Some, yes." He sweeps his tongue along my skin. "Salty ones."

I moan as his arms wrap around my waist.

"I prefer the company of a few over being with masses of people. The ranch has a constant buzz of activity in the summer. I look forward to when the snow comes and we drop down to a skeleton staff. When I need quiet, I head into the mountains."

"By yourself?"

"Best company I know." He gently tugs my braid.

"Far from the applause of the crowd?"

"You've probably figured out by now, I'm not into stardom. Or crowds." He gently encourages me to turn with pressure on my hips. "I prefer one on one."

"Me too," I whisper, unable to break the spell he's created with his hands and mouth.

TWENTY-NINE

JUSTIN

A BIG PART of me thought Zoe would be pissed because I misled her about our accommodations. If she is, she's hiding it well.

Better to lie about sleeping in a tent and reveal a cabin than the other way around. Like stuffing your jeans. How does that help the situation? Once you take off your pants, the truth is going to disappoint. I've never understood it. And obviously, I've never done it.

I could take her right here on the kitchen counter, but there's more to the tour, including the master bedroom with the huge four poster king bed.

We can have sex in every room in the house, including the kitchen, the sauna, and definitely under the stars on the deck. Out here, with no one around for miles, we have the ultimate privacy, freedom to be ourselves. And that is worth more than any money sitting in the bank.

I press against her, caressing her lips with mine in a slow, soft kiss full of promises. Tonight, there's no rush. Nowhere else for us to be.

Her fingers brush past my waist before resting on my ass. I

chuckle against her mouth as she pulls me closer, opening her legs to settle me between them.

"I'm going to be honest, I've been a little obsessed with your ass since the first rodeo." Her breath mingles with mine as she speaks.

"Seems only fair." I trail my hands above her waist and let them rest on her ribs, right below the fullness of her breasts.

"I blame the chaps." She kisses me. Or tries to, but I'm laughing and our mouths fumble against each other.

Leaning away, I ask, "Excuse me?"

"Don't pretend you don't know." Her beautiful dark eyes narrow as she stares into mine. "You know."

"I'm not sure I do." My cheek twitches as I fight a smile. "Standard protection. Like a helmet. Or a vest."

I drag one of her hands away from my ass and pull it to my chest, placing it over my heart.

Her lashes flutter as she quickly blinks. Staring at her hand, she exhales a shaky breath. I love her reactions to my words, to my touch.

"I'm more than what's framed by a pair of chaps," I whisper the words as I kiss the corner of her mouth. "But if you're curious to see more, all you have to do is ask."

Her groan makes me laugh. "Too thick?"

When her hips roll into mine, she responds, "No, feels perfect."

"You." I give her a peck. "Are. Perfect." Each word is emphasized with another kiss. "Come with me."

I lead her upstairs to the master bedroom. The view up here is even better and she immediately steps closer to the windows.

"I'd never get tired of this view." She presses her hand against the glass.

"Me neither." I follow behind her.

Relief and happiness flood my veins. To have her here with

me after the uncertainty between us the past few weeks, means everything to me.

I told her I'm not a patient man, but when she was taking time to figure out her heart, I learned the power of patience. And faith that she'd come back to me.

"Zoe," I whisper, nerves adding a rough edge to my voice.

Her eyes shift to mine as she faces me. In their depth, I can see her joy and own happiness. My chest swells with pride. I didn't lie when I told her nothing matters in the world more to me than her happiness.

Her smile brightens her face as she stares at me. I lean into the touch of her hand on my cheek. When she presses her other hand over my heart, I lose control of my restraint.

It's too soon to feel this way.

It's crazy to think this is real.

Love is a wild thing we can't control. Only a fool would try to tame the human heart.

I blink away the tide of emotion behind my eyes as she leads me over to the big bed. We quietly strip off our clothes, until we're bare before each other.

In her studio, I wanted to prove myself worthy of her. I still needed to reassure myself she could love all of me, not just the fantasy. Now, as I lay her down and crawl over her, I know she's mine as surely as I know I belong to her.

Today, I make love to her slowly. We have enough time to explore each other until I know her body as well as my own. Outside the mountains deepens into purple and indigo as the sun slips away.

There will be more sunrises and early mornings greeted with golden light. Time to discover new places in our hearts where new love dwells.

When I feel her getting close to release, I chase after my own, wanting to break apart and come back together at the same time. Her face fills with beautiful, unrestrained bliss as she comes undone. I will never get enough of her fierce beauty, her untamable passion.

EPILOGUE

A MAN WHO feeds me cake for breakfast after making love to me all night can't be real. But he is.

Justin Garrison is the most dangerous kind of man.

He's a good person.

He doesn't play games.

He owns his mistakes.

Plus, he makes a pair of chaps sinful.

I might have fallen for a cowboy, but it's the man beneath the hat who has my heart.

Across the crowded gallery, I find his soulful eyes. He gives me a slow, sexy smile that makes his eyes crinkle.

My body zings and he's all the way on the other side of the room.

I grin at him and watch as happiness spreads across his face.

"Quit making googly eyes at your man." Sage nudges me with her sharp elbow.

"I can't help it. Have you seen how handsome he is?" Tonight, Justin's in dark jeans and the fitted black shirt he wore on our first date. And yes, he's wearing a championship silver buckle.

Around him men in suits look like penguin robots.

Now that his hair's grown out more and started to wave,

I'm barely able to restrain myself from running my fingers through it constantly.

"You're drooling. Right here." Sage dabs her finger at the corner of my mouth.

I tear my gaze from Justin. "Why are you being annoying?"

"Because you're in love and it's fun to tease you." Mae hands me a glass of champagne.

"Tell us about your art," Mara says from the other side of Sage. "Why is everything broken?"

"Because the flaws and scars are what make it beautiful." I sip my champagne.

Surrounding us are my sculptures from Ashcroft. Displayed on white plinths, highlighted with beautiful lighting, each porcelain anatomically correct human heart has been shattered and put back together. Lines of silver fill the gaps and cracks of the breaks.

The idea came to me the afternoon Justin visited my studio. When we had sex for the first time and my heart began to heal.

Never again will I be the girl who loved a boy who only promised a life of safety and security. My heart bears the scars of that mistake, but new love fills them, strengthening me.

"Why silver?" Mae asks.

"For Aspen's past as a mining town. For the mountains and the veins of silver hiding beneath rock and dirt."

And for the man I love. A Colorado cowboy who loves this place with his whole heart.

We haven't said the words out loud yet, but I see them in his eyes and feel them when his lips press against my skin.

Zoe, surrounded by her beautiful artwork and being celebrated by her friends, glows with happiness. In a flowy black dress and colorful, silky wrap covering her shoulders, she looks the part of the hottest new artist in town. I've heard brides and pregnant women glow, but she is luminous. Creating art and sharing it with the world could be similar to a wedding or birth, I suppose.

I stare at her across the crowded museum as she laughs with her girlfriends. Her loose, wavy hair is a Siren's call to me. All evening my eyes have followed her as she's greeted collectors and talked about her sculptures. This is her night and she shines like the brightest star in the room.

Red dots mark most of her works. My grandmother bought two. Mine sits at home on a shelf in the bedroom. I made her promise to give me the one she based on the broken one. The heart she shattered against the wall out of anger and fear.

She sees the beauty in the fragments. In the cracks, I see strength and healing.

Before Zoe, I didn't realize how much my walls of protection had isolated me from living a full life. I believed living on my own terms equaled liberty, but I'd created a different kind of cage around my heart. Loving Zoe has healed me.

I excuse myself from the group of Ashcroft members. With a purpose to my step, I stride directly over to Zoe.

"Sorry, ladies, but I need to steal your friend." I beam at the group, letting my eyes linger on Zoe's beautiful face. "I might bring her back, but can't make any promises."

Sage and Mara softly giggle as I loop Zoe's hand through my elbow.

"Where are we going?" Zoe asks, as I lead us through the crowd toward the doors.

"I missed you." Outside, the rooftop garden is mostly empty in the cool October air. "And I missed seeing the stars."

We wander along the path to a quiet corner near the edge. For a few moments, we both stare over the buildings. The city lights dim the starlight, but a few brighter dots sparkle near a half moon.

"It smells like snow." She tilts her head back and gazes into the night sky. "I wonder if it's snowing back home."

"It might be. Are you cold?" I don't have a jacket to give her, so instead I wrap my arm around her shoulder.

Facing me, she curls into me in a tight embrace. "Thank you."

"For keeping you warm?"

"For all of this." She softly touches her lips to mine. "You make my life better simply by being part of it."

"This is all you. Your talent. Your fierce bravery to follow your dream."

When she gazes into my eyes, I know this is the moment to knock down my walls.

"I love you," I say, filling the space between each word with promises and vows to mean it for the rest of our lives.

"I love you," I repeat into the silence because it's the truth. As real as the mountains we call home and the endless sky above.

I feel the push of air as she exhales into the stillness. My words float between us, suspended in the air, waiting.

Her fingers press harder against my heart and tears dot her dark lashes. "I love you. As true as your heart beats, mine is yours."

"I'll take good care of it. I promise. For every new sunrise and starry night. For as long as I'm breathing," I swear to her with millions of stars as our witness, "I belong to you."

A NOTE FROM DAISY

Thank you for reading *Wild for You!*

I hope you enjoyed Zoe and Justin's story. I had the best time writing this and love Zoe as much as I swoon over Justin.

The idea of a cowboy and an artist was sparked during a visit to Snowmass Village, Colorado in June this year. Visits to the Anderson Ranch Arts Center and the T-Lazy-7 Ranch inspired the idea of a city girl falling for a Colorado cowboy. Snowmass does have a weekly rodeo full of bull riding, bronco bucking cowboys. Giddy up!

If you haven't read the other two standalones in the Love with Altitude series, please check out *Next to You* and *Crazy Over You*. Click to the end of this book for the buy-links for all of my current titles.

I appreciate you taking the time to write an honest review and sharing it on Goodreads or your favorite retailer. Reviews and personal recommendations are the best ways to get the word out about books we enjoy.

To keep up with my latest news and upcoming releases, sing up for my *mailing list*.

xo

Daisy

ABOUT DAISY

DAISY PRESCOTT IS the USA Today bestselling author of contemporary romantic comedies, including Modern Love Stories, the Wingmen series, and the Love with Altitude series, as well as the Bewitched series of magical Halloween shorts.

Daisy currently lives in a real life Stars Hollow in the Boston suburbs with her husband, their rescue dog Mulder, and an indeterminate number of imaginary house goats. When not writing, she can be found in the garden or kitchen, lost in a good book, or on social media, usually talking about books, bearded men, and sloths.

www.daisyprescott.com

www.twitter.com/Daisy_Prescott

www.facebook.com/daisyprescottauthorpage

www.instagram.com/daisyprescott

ACKNOWLEDGMENTS

AS ALWAYS, FIRST thank you is to my husband for supporting this wild life. And by wild I mean living with me when I'm on deadline, always in pajamas, or workout clothes, unsure if the dishes in the dishwasher are clean, the dog's been fed, or what's for dinner. It takes a special kind of partner to be married to a writer. Your unwavering belief in me and support of this dream mean the world to me. Our brainstorming sessions, your first feedback, and straight talk about how men really think make my books better. Thank you for being mine. I'm so lucky to walk through this life with you. I love you more than tacos.

Thank you to my family for always making Snowmass feel like home. Our time together inspired this story and the settings. All names have been changed to protect our secrets.

To all of my author friends and colleagues in the Indie world, you continue to inspire me every day. I'm honored to be in the company of so many talented and amazing women.

To my reader-friends in Daisyland, thank you for being a part of my daily life. I love our little group. I wish I could give you all an Awesome Reader Cake. MJ Fryer, thank you for being tough. Erika Gutermuth, thank you for always believing in me.

SM Lumetta, thank you for the beautiful cover and series branding. This cover makes me swoon every time I look at it. Christine, thank you for turning words into beautiful books and your continued kindness. Jenn, thank you for designing beautiful swag. Fiona, your graphics rock. All of you are truly talented, and I'm lucky to work with you

Big thanks to my team, who keep me focused on the forest through the trees: Fiona Fischer, my amazing assistant who is an expert cat herder behind the scenes; my editor, Melissa

Ringsted at There for You Editing; proofreaders, Marla Esposito of Proofing with Style and Elli Reid; my publicist, Jessica Estep at Inkslinger PR; Jeananna and Kylie at Give Me Books; my agent, Meire Dias at Bookcase Literary Agency; and KP Simmon at Inkslinger PR, for handholding and ass-kicking as needed. I say the same thing with every book, but I couldn't do this without you. Thank you all for being amazing. I love you more than cake.

Biggest thanks of all to you, dear readers, for continuing to buy and read my books. You inspire me to keep writing. Your reviews and word of mouth about books you love are invaluable. Thank you for spending your time with my stories.

Hearing from my readers is one of the best parts of publishing. I can be reached on social media or at *daisyauthor@gmail.com*.

xo
Daisy

www.ingramcontent.com/pod-product-compliance
Lightning Source LLC
Chambersburg PA
CBHW021007120726
47905CB00009B/2889